Baby

BABY

Joseph Monninger

Front Street
Asheville, North Carolina

To our dogs, here, and gone

Printed in China
Designed by Helen Robinson
First edition

Library of Congress Cataloging-in-Publication Data

Monninger, Joseph.
Baby / Joseph Monninger. — 1st ed.
p. cm.
Summary: Fifteen-year-old Baby's last chance at foster care is with the Potters, and while she likes them and enjoys learning to race their sled dogs, she feels she should go back on the streets with her boyfriend if she cannot find the mother who has deserted her again.
ISBN-13: 978-1-59078-502-7 (hardcover : alk. paper)
[1. Foster home care—Fiction. 2. Sled dogs—Fiction. 3. Sled dog racing—Fiction. 4. Dogs—Fiction. 5. Social service—Fiction. 6. New Hampshire—Fiction.] I. Title.
PZ7.M7537Bab 2007
[Fic]—dc22

2006101749

Front Street
An Imprint of Boyds Mills Press, Inc.
815 Church Street
Honesdale, Pennsylvania 18431

What but the wolf's tooth whittled so fine
the fleet limbs of the antelope?
Robinson Jeffers

Baby

1

She smelled like peaches.

I had to wonder: did she want to smell like peaches, or did she go out and buy some ridiculous spray from one of those candle shops and shoot it all round her little Jetta? She looked butchy to me: one of those big fat dyke women who think all girls possess an instant understanding of each other. She didn't trust me, either, because she kept looking over, touching the radio with one hand, listening for a second, raising her eyebrows to see if it was okay with me (it wasn't), then going on to the next song.

"So tell me," she said, "does everyone call you Baby? Was that like a nickname from way back?"

I didn't look at her.

She kept pushing buttons.

Cindy, that was her name.

"I was just wondering what you prefer to be called," she said. "You know, to introduce you."

I looked out the window. I found if I leaned just a little out of the window, just a scratch, the cold touched the stud on my nose and turned it bright white. The cold passed right through it and traveled up my nasal passage. I had never known that could happen and I liked it.

"We should be there in, like, ten minutes. Maybe fifteen. I told the Potters we'd be there around two. We'll get you settled in while there's still some daylight."

The cold kept climbing the stud. I leaned a little farther out. Mountains rose up out of the dull afternoon on either side of us. New Hampshire. Cow-freaking Hampshire.

Cindy pulled the Jetta over and I knew it was time for the talk.

They always give a talk.

They think if they can just get through to you. They think if they say just the right words everything will become crystal clear.

She reached over and turned down the radio.

"The Potters," she said, "are some of the best foster parents we have. The very best."

She stared ahead when she said this as if she had revealed some big fat secret. The car bumped a little on its idle. Cheap car, cheap perfume. That's what I thought. I wanted a cigarette so bad I could hardly stand it. Sometimes I can talk myself into believing I am smoking just by sucking in air. It sounds crazy, I know, but if you curl your tongue and inhale, sometimes it works. I reached over and turned up the radio.

She turned it down.

I almost had to laugh.

I faked turning it up and her hand shot out.

I turned to the window and had to put my fist next to my mouth to keep from laughing. So predictable. They all are.

"The Potters take only one kid a year. They stay with that kid no matter what. Do you understand me? *They* never back out. Only the kids back out. They are committed to you no matter what. Do you know what that means?"

I didn't say anything.

"That means you can be as big an asshole as you like and they are still going to stay with you. You can't turn them off. Nothing you can do will make them hate you. That's their special therapy."

"Well, screw them," I said. "I don't need therapy."

She didn't say anything.

We sat quietly for a while.

"They're older, but don't let that fool you. They live pretty close to the earth. They don't go in for a lot of frills."

I looked out the window. I would have done just about anything for a cigarette.

Bobby says: *People try to fence you in. That's what school is about, that's what jobs are about, that's the whole process of the world. Every year you live they take away more freedom.*

I knew it was going to be *that* kind of house. I knew it. I knew the trees would be groomed and cut nicely, and the lawn would be tidy, and the bushes wouldn't be crazy or anything. It looked like a Hobbit house. White-and-black shutters, a roof that had different dormers and things. It was like a *This Old House* kind of house.

"We're here," Cindy said.

I waited in the car while Cindy climbed out. She bent down to see me through the windshield, her face all filled with phony concern. Was I coming out? What was going on? I could have laughed again. Then she did her butchy waddle up to the front steps. She knocked on the door but kept turning back to make sure I hadn't run away again. That's what's so stupid about social work people. They think you have no brains at all, that you will run away like a complete idiot. I wanted to tell her I wouldn't run away until I had it all lined up. Until I had heard from Bobby. I wanted to tell her she wouldn't know I was gone until I was.

The door opened. The house door. And a tall woman with gray hair let Cindy inside. The woman stood for a second in the doorway. She looked like an old hippie woman, one of those VW burnouts who used to follow the Dead. My mom was a little like that, so I knew the type.

Then Cindy went inside and the gray-haired woman came out. She wore jeans and a black sweater and a down vest. Birkenstocks. I almost started to laugh again. I mean, how perfect. She was the kind of woman who was probably into social causes and political action. She had a big walk. Purposeful and straight. She probably prided herself on her posture.

She came and stood next to my door.

I lifted my elbow up and clicked the door lock down.

"Yank you very much," I said.

Then the woman did a strange thing. For a second I knew she was trying to figure things out. Here was this girl she hadn't even met locked in a car. The car sat in her driveway. Most people, most adults anyway, would have tried to open the door. Or they would have pointed at me and made a "roll down the window" sign. Or they would have spoken with a big, loud mouth: "Heeeellloooo, my name isssssss ..." Blah blah blah.

But the woman didn't do that.

She sized things up. Then, very carefully, she wrote something in the window frost. She was smart about that, too, because she leaned over and wrote it on the back window first. I didn't turn around. Then she came around and wrote on the driver's side. Then on the windshield. Then on the window right next to me. I gave her the finger and let it slowly rotate as she went around the car.

But before I could even see what she wrote, she left. She headed back to the house.

On the back window she wrote: E–2.1

On the driver's-side window she wrote: S–3.7

On the windshield she wrote: W–1.6

On the window next to me she wrote: N–4.8

It took me a while to figure it out. I had actually to think like a Birkenstock- wearing, gray-ponytail type to get it. I figured she lived way the hell out in Cow Hampshire and she was into the earth and all that crap, and then I got it. She had written down the compass points. The numbers indicated how many miles to the next house. It couldn't have been anything else, I realized.

And all I could think of is what Bobby would have said. He would have said, *This is a big freaking teachable moment.* I was supposed to understand some greater meaning. Teachers are always doing that. They look at you like this is the most important thing anyone ever said.

Older people, Bobby says, *always think they have the right to try to teach you something. But that's just one person using his or her power over another.* He says the only things we draft people for in America are the military and the public school systems.

I pulled down my pants. I know that sounds crazy, but I hadn't even had a minute to see the tattoo. That's where they finally tracked me down—in Screaming Needles outside of Worchester. It was kind of funny, too, because I was sitting with my ass up in the air, letting Wan tattoo an Asian tiger on my right cheek, when Child Services came in. Somebody had squealed. Wan turned all white because he was in big freaking trouble, tattooing an under-aged, and all that kind of crap. I didn't even see Bobby. He had gone to get munchies, and it was like three in the morning, and somebody must have tipped them. But there I am with my butt in the air, and this cop and Cindy come in. The tiger was almost finished. It was small, but, anyway, this ridiculous conversation followed about whether I should be allowed to finish it. I know that sounds nuts, but what's the point of having half a tattoo? That's what I told them. They said no way. I knew, though, that Cindy was trying to be understanding and she didn't know what to do. She looked at it fast and told Wan to finish the damn thing. So he did. Then they bandaged it and took me, and it hurt like hell to sit when they ran me down to the juvey center.

So now, in the car, this was really the first chance I'd had to see the tattoo. I pulled my jeans down and knelt on the passenger seat and crooked the rearview mirror around so I could see down. It was hard to figure out the design because it was still raw and the angle was awkward, but I liked what I saw. Wan had used a lot of blue and green, so it made my skin look sick. He had also made the tiger stripes spell out "Bobby," at least he said so, but you couldn't really see it. I examined it for a while, then slipped my pants back up.

By that time I realized it was getting damn cold in the car.

I guess that was the message. No one was going to force me to come in. I had the choice to sit in the cold or walk one of those compass points and find whatever I could, or I could come inside. Big moment. That's what Bobby says. He says everyone has watched too many movies, so everyone thinks life is going to be like that. Sound tracks in your head. Big family reunions. And happy ever after. He says movies kill you more than anything, because they always make your life look like crap. Either that, or you keep waiting for that big movie moment to arrive and it never does.

So this is what Bobby would have called someone trying to wedge a movie moment into my life. The gray-haired lady wanted to be like the Korean guy in *The Karate Kid.* Big lessons.

"Screw her," I said aloud. And I sat until it was too damn cold and I had to pee.

2

They had a woodstove going. I smelled it as soon as I stepped inside. And someone had started making cookies, too, and that was supposed to be for me. It was supposed to be a big deal to have fresh cookies baking, I knew, like my mom had never baked cookies for me. Bite me, I would have said if anyone had been around.

The house had low ceilings with the beams exposed. Of course. And wood paneling covered the walls. Wide pine floors. Antiques. It was the kind of house that chatters when you walk because they have glass and knickknacks everywhere. And a clock ticked somewhere. A big, heavy sound, like every minute in this house meant something.

I had to pee bad.

I looked around. Voices came from the back of the house, probably the kitchen. I figured they had heard me come in, but they had decided to play it cool. I was supposed to come to them. Bullshit stuff. I walked on my toes to the left. A hallway. I looked down, then walked to my right. The entryway opened onto a TV kind of family room with a fireplace and a couple of skylights. A baby grand piano sat next to a bay window.

I went back to the hallway, still on my toes, and walked down. I figured the bathroom had to be off the hallway, and I was right.

It was a pretty big room with another skylight, but the toilet threw me for a second. It came up to my waist, almost, and looked like a clothes dryer. Sort of. When I opened the toilet lid, I nearly gagged. The inside held a bunch of what looked like human crap and wood chips. Except you couldn't really tell it was crap—it was just like an old outhouse. I didn't have a choice. I sat on it, did what I had to do, and my eye caught a sign next to the toilet. It explained that the Potters had decided to use a composting toilet, that regular toilets used one to two gallons of water per flush, that the septic pumped into the earth wasn't good, and blah blah blah. Freaking hippie-dippie shit. At least the toilet didn't smell. I gave them that much.

I opened the medicine cabinet. They had cleaned it out. Figured. But the hippie woman had some makeup behind the sink, so I put on some lipstick for the hell of it. I smeared it on hard. Plum Passion. How freaking corny. Then I drew little zigzags on my cheeks with the lipstick. I looked like an Indian. I made my lips even bigger, like the way my friend Macey used to do it. She used to get all nutty about makeup. She put on so much in department stores they would kick her out. She'd go up and down the mall and smear on some from each store until finally they told her to cut it out. It was funny. Every time Macey headed for the makeup department, some old broad would jump out from behind a counter and head her off.

I looked in the mirror. "Trick-or-treat," I said.

I almost started laughing when I saw Cindy's eyes bug when she caught a glimpse of my makeup job. I walked into the kitchen and stood in the doorway. The woodstove sat on a round brick shelf between two sliding doors. A big deck was out behind it. Birds flew to a feeder nailed onto the railing of the deck.

The man saw me first. He looked to be about seventy, gray-haired, and with those kind of blue eyes that bother you almost to stare into. He wore a plaid shirt and jeans and a pair of hiking boots. He was big, though, about six five or so. He filled the room, and I wondered if he had to duck through doorways most of his life. I watched to see if his eyes registered my makeup. They probably did, but he didn't make a big deal of it.

"Fred Potter," he said, holding out his hand. "You must be Baby."

We shook. His hand was enormous!

Then his wife stood and introduced herself as Mary.

No one said anything about the makeup. Mary offered me cider and kermits. Cindy made room on the couch and I sat next to her. Mary had a silk-covered easy chair and Fred had a winged-back chair. I admit I liked them well enough. You couldn't really hate them. It probably sounds crazy, but they seemed perfectly adapted to their environment. *Their* environment, though. They would have folded in a second with Bobby and Macey and the rest. But right where they lived, with the woodstove pushing heat, and the cider, and the beamed house—I had no beef with them.

I sat.

"Try the kermits," Cindy said. "They're amazing."

I took one. Mary poured me a glass of cider.

Cindy said, "This cider is made from apples on their property. They have one hundred and sixty acres."

I bit into the kermit. It tasted like cinnamon and something else I couldn't name. No raisins. I hate raisins.

I drank some cider.

Then no one said anything.

"Here are the rules," Cindy said after a while. "I want to review them in front of the Potters so that we're all clear. I don't want any misunderstandings, okay?"

I kept eating my kermit. It was good.

"The rules are simple. The Potters are in loco parentis, meaning they have parental rights over you temporarily. That's important because it gives them authority to set up the household the way they deem fit. Okay? So that's the first rule."

A log shifted in the woodstove. Fred got up and swung a door open and poked at it for a second. Then he added a log, shut the door, and sat back down. He moved pretty well for an old guy, so I had to revise his age down to about sixty or so.

"You are not to leave the house without the Potters' permission. As we agreed, you are going to work for your GED. You will take the exam when you feel ready. I will visit once a week to review how things are going. You may call me if you need something, but otherwise the phone is to be used at the Potters' discretion. That's true of anything in the house—TV, stereo, and so on."

"We don't have a television," Mary said.

I looked at her.

She looked back. She shrugged.

"Obviously," Cindy said, "no drugs, drinking, or smoking. No driving any vehicles. No visitors. No Internet surfing to inappropriate sites."

"We don't have the Internet," Mary said.

She shrugged again.

"And I guess that's about everything," Cindy said. "We try to use common sense. The Potters, as I explained, are experienced. They have done foster care before. We've never had a problem interpreting the rules. Any questions from anyone?"

Fred shook his head.

Mary looked at me. "Would you like to see your room?" she asked.

"This used to be a tack room for horses," Mary said. "Long ago, this was a working farm, so they needed someplace to store all the horse equipment. You can see the hooks and things on the wall there."

It was a funny room but nice. What I liked best about it was you took three steps down to the bed. Back in the tack-room day, the bed space would have been on a porch. But that had all been closed in with barn boards. They left a large window, and that was a cute touch. You could be on the bed and look out. What I also liked was that the room didn't try to be all girly. It was just a room, probably a guest room, but it had a comfortable feeling.

A stack of clothes waited on the foot of the bed. They looked like work clothes. Jeans, underwear, socks, a pair of Doc Martens boots. Three sweaters. Mary had also included a new toothbrush, toothpaste, and towels.

"Cindy told me your size," Mary said. "She guessed at it, anyway. You can always take things back."

"I won't wear that shit," I said.

"You don't have to."

"I'm not like you," I said. "Not country."

"Okay," she said.

"I'm not."

"Okay. You don't have to be. Sometimes, though, we do work around here and these clothes come in handy. You can put them away and see."

"The Doc Martens are okay," I said.

"Well, there's a start," she said.

We stood there for a second, not doing much. It wasn't a nervous kind of silence. Mary looked calm. She *was* tall, I realized, maybe over six feet. And she had big hands. I was living with freaking giants.

"Is this the room you always use?" I asked.

"For what?"

"For kids. Foster kids."

"Yes," she said.

"How many have you had?"

"Oh, probably about a dozen. We retired up here. Fred was a lawyer once upon a time."

"Where?"

"In New York."

"So this is what you do now?"

"No," she said, "this is one thing that we do."

"What's the main thing you do?"

"Run dogs," she said.

People give you something to get something, Bobby says. *That's the way of the world. You can't even do a good act, because as soon as you do it, it makes you feel good. Doing good is as selfish as anything else.*

Cindy came in the room when Mary left. Cindy talked quiet, way back in her throat. She looked at the clothes, then at me.

"Didn't I say they were nice?" she said.

"They're okay," I said. "I'm not staying very long."

"You don't have to. Just relax for a little while until things get sorted out."

I said, "Did you get hold of my mom?"

She shook her head.

"Why not?" I asked.

"She wasn't at the last address. We don't know where to find her. We're looking."

"Screw her, then," I said.

"That's helpful," Cindy said. "Do you have any ideas where she might have gone?"

"She goes south when it gets cold. She's with the biker guy."

"Harry?"

"Yeah."

"Do you know his last name?"

"Schmidt or something. German name, he said."

"Harry Schmidt, then. We'll run his name. It's a big country, Baby. If someone wants to stay gone, they can."

"My mom will be back," I said.

"I'm sure she will."

She said it, of course, in a way to let me know she didn't think Mom was coming back anytime soon. She was probably right, but to hell with her. I was sick of Cindy and all the do-gooders. They always had this private place, this judging place, that made them look at whatever you were going to do and dismiss it.

I took the clothes and put them on the dresser. Then I let myself fall face-forward on the bed. I put my head in the pillows. I felt tired and sleepy. I always like a nap in the afternoon. But mostly I wanted Cindy to get out of there and leave me alone. I knew she wouldn't. I knew she had to give me a pep talk. Cindy was big on pep talks.

She opened the bathroom door and looked inside. Then she put the stack of clothes away in the dresser drawers. She hummed a little under her breath. You could go crazy listening to someone hum. That's the truth.

"This is a great room," she said. "You could be happy here if you let yourself."

When I didn't respond, she sat on the bed.

I didn't move. I tried to make my breathing sound like I was asleep.

"Baby," she said, "you're running out of chances. You are. I'm sorry, I know you don't want to hear it, but you are. The judge isn't going to let you float around to foster homes much longer. Next stop will be in the juvey center."

She didn't say anything else. Not for a while.

"You're smart, Baby. You could be anything you want. You've got a first-class mind. Somewhere down in your heart you know stealing and sleeping on the streets aren't going to bring you any-place good. You know that. You're too smart not to know that. It may seem like fun in the short run, but it can't last. And winter is here. Ask yourself next time you want to leave, 'Where am I going?'

Where are you really going? Think about sleeping in those awful places you slept. The abandoned buildings. The back of U-Haul trucks. How long could that go on? Where does it end? I think you know the answer to that."

I didn't say anything. I curled my tongue and breathed through it slowly. I drew my breath in like a cigarette inhale, then let it out slow.

"The Potters are good people. They won't mess with you. They don't want anything from you. They've raised their own boy and they've worked with other foster kids. Just take a little time, okay? Don't fight quite so much. Just take a breather."

Then she stood and went out. She closed the door.

3

Somebody put his tongue in my ear.

It freaked me out and I sat up so fast I had no idea where I was.

It was dark out and the room was cold.

I had been having a dream, but the dream split and suddenly I couldn't remember where I was. Sleeping on the street, you hardly ever let yourself sleep deeply and certainly not deep enough to allow some perv to sneak up and put his tongue in your ear.

But I wasn't on the street.

I took a second to remember that.

Something breathed in the room. Little by little I remembered where I was. The door to my room was open, and light came in through the crack. I heard jazz playing somewhere and smelled the woodstove. I also smelled something else, something cooking, and my stomach started to gnaw.

I put my hand out. A dog licked it.

"Jesus Christ," I said.

I had no idea how to find the light switch. I swung my legs out and put my hand against the dog. It felt enormous. It had a coat like a shag rug, and its breath smelled of kibbles.

"Get out of here," I said, but it kept breathing on me.

I went to the door and opened it wider to let light in. Then I fished around on the wall until I found the light switch. I hit it. I drew in my breath when I saw the dog.

It was a wolf, not a dog.

It was so scary, it was cool.

"Whoa," I said.

It looked at me. His eyes were blue. And his coat was thicker than anything I had ever seen.

Mary suddenly pushed in the door from the other side.

"Sorry," she said, "I was afraid he'd wake you."

"What's his name?" I asked.

"Sebastian."

"Is he a wolf?"

"Part wolf. A hybrid. We have a lot of dogs around, but Sebastian is the alpha dog. What Sebastian says goes."

"I believe it," I said.

"We bring the dogs in to socialize them. It's a rotation. Sebastian comes in every night. He sleeps in the living room. We walk him through town when we run errands on Saturdays. We figure if anyone had a notion of breaking in here, Sebastian would convince them otherwise."

"He'd kill them," I said. "He's cool."

"He wouldn't do anything, actually. He's a fluff ball. Come here, boy."

Sebastian moved over to her. His back came above my waist. I had never seen a dog like him. Not in real life.

"Jesus," I said.

I put my hand on his head. His ears pricked up, then sagged. He leaned a little against my leg.

"Dinner will be ready in a few minutes," Mary said. "We're veggies, so I hope you won't mind. You have time to jump in the shower if you want."

"I might," I said.

"Good," she said, and went out.

She didn't offer to take Sebastian with her.

Here's one cool thing about the Potters.

They gave me a glass of wine with dinner.

They could probably get in a ton of trouble for doing it, but they didn't make a big deal out of it. They had one bottle of red wine on the table. It wasn't a big jug of wine, and they didn't have a drink before dinner. They just served wine with the meal. Simple. And they didn't seem to care that I was only fifteen.

"You always give kids wine?" I asked.

"Always," Fred said.

He laughed. He laughed easily and from way down in his chest.

"We gave our son wine as he grew up," Mary said. "We figured it's silly to hold things back if you want to teach the benefits of moderation. He may have drunk to excess a couple times at college and so on, but not as bad as some kids do. A little wine is a good thing. That's what I believe."

"Awesome," I said.

They were okay. The food was okay. The house was pretty cool. Sebastian was the coolest, because he sat against me. He didn't beg or bother me, but he stayed next to me and kept an eye out. I still couldn't get over his stare. He appeared as though he could rip your guts out, but he was gentle as could be. Weird.

Then a strange thing happened. Way outside, I heard a howl. At first I thought I was hearing things. Then a few more voices blended. I looked at Mary. Then at Fred. Then right underneath me, Sebastian put his head back and let out the loudest sound I had ever heard. I had to cover my ears. The howl had all the strange emotion you heard in wolf cries. Of course, I had never heard a true-life wolf cry, but I knew one thing: hearing it on TV was nothing like the real thing.

Slowly the howls from outside grew and grew and then began to fade. Sebastian stayed right with them. He put his head back and bullfrogged his throat.

"Yours?" I asked them when the dogs finally quieted.

They nodded.

Here's the thing about the Potters: they live inside *and* outside.

For instance, right after dinner we all put on jackets to go outside. When you live down in Massachusetts, you make a big deal about going outside. People put on jackets and scarves and all that crap. But the Potters had about a dozen mackinaws, these big, warm jackets on hooks next to the door. And they had muck boots you could slide into without any trouble. So I guess the transition from inside to outside was so simple it made it all feel natural and easy. I liked that.

I followed Fred out. Frost covered the lawn, and some sleet fell. Mary brought her teacup. I was aware this was a big moment—one of those things Bobby would have scoffed at. But at the same time, he hadn't met Sebastian or heard those dogs howl. I still couldn't believe what I had heard. It seemed like the Russian fairy tales my mom used to read me.

Sebastian led us across a white meadow. He looked beautiful

trotting in moonlight. The Potters had a lot of land, because you couldn't see any lights anywhere besides the house. All darkness. All pines. The stars had already pushed out, and I had to admit it was pretty. I thought of a night that Bobby and I spent on top of a milk truck. It had been parked on a vacant lot, down by a 7-Eleven on Black Avenue, and at first we had climbed inside. But it was hot in there, and so Bobby boosted me up on top. Then he threw up our sleeping bags and scrambled up. We spread them out and lay up on top, just smoking cigarettes and talking. I fell asleep twice, and each time I woke, Bobby was still talking. I could see the stars and no other lights, and I had a feeling that I was infinitely small, horribly small, and that the top of the truck was really the surface of a flyswatter and we were going to be smashed. And it felt like we were rising up up up up up into the stars, and then Bobby's voice pushed us back down, little by little, and he knew it too. He knew if he stopped talking we would be crushed on the surface of the truck, so he talked and I slept, and when I woke, the top of the truck was so hot it burned our hands and feet as we climbed down.

"How many do you have?" I asked.

"Sixteen," Fred said. "Two six-dog teams and two spares. And we have Sebastian and the puppy."

I don't care what Bobby said. It was a moment.

We stood in the cold meadow and stared at the dogs. They stood in wire mesh pens, all of them right up against it to see us. At first they barked like mad. Then they quieted and began whining a little. Then nothing except their white breath and the gleaming eyes looking at me, looking at us.

I had to force myself to take a step back. Mentally, I mean. They had a large barnlike thing in the corner of the field. Part of the dog pens stretched under the overhang, but the other part jutted out into the open air. A door opened onto each pen. Some of the pens held two dogs, others just one. The dogs slept in rubber barrels, the insides lined with straw.

Each cage had a sign with the dogs' names.

Muppin, Charlie, Willow, Buster, Rocky, Bruce, Smoke, Lefty, Poor Boy, Lady Gray, Earth Monkey, Bob, Teddy Roosevelt, and Second Boss.

"You can pet them," Mary said.

Fred went to each cage and put his knuckles against the mesh. The dogs sniffed and whined to be petted. I moved forward slowly. They looked as lean as knife blades, these dogs.

"Wow," I said.

"They're Alaskan sled dogs," Fred said. "Part Siberians. Part hound, some of them. They can go distances, but they really are suited to sprint. We race them in the New England Sled Dog championships. It goes all winter."

I put my fingers to the mesh as Fred had done. The dogs jumped and sniffed my hands. Then Mary showed me where to get dog biscuits from a little cupboard, and we fed them each a treat. They ate with quick, delicate bites. They swirled in front of me and I couldn't begin to remember which was which.

Laika stood in the puppy cage.

If I live to be one hundred years old, I'll remember seeing Laika the first time.

She was white, pure white. The other dogs had mixed colors, but not Laika.

When I came to her pen, she lifted her paw and pressed it against the mesh. We held hands like that. She studied me. Neither one of us moved to pull away.

"Laika's coming inside tonight. It's supposed to get cold," Mary said. "And we've been socializing her. Getting her used to people."

"How cold?" Fred asked.

He pulled at a bent piece of mesh at the bottom of one of the cages. It bent right back into position. He had his mitten between his teeth, so when he asked, "How cold?" it came out "Hwcold?"

"Ten degrees. Snow tomorrow."

I could hardly take my eyes off Laika. She looked like a husky—or what I thought was a husky—with pale blue eyes and pointed ears. Fred didn't make a big deal of letting her out. He flipped the latch and the metal door swung open. Laika flew out, then flattened almost immediately when she spotted Sebastian. She lowered her rear and peed. Sebastian hardly noticed.

Fred said, "Well, I guess she knows who the boss is."

"Would Sebastian hurt her?" I asked.

"No, Baby. Sebastian has never been in a fight of any kind. Who would even try him? He never learned to be mean."

Laika ran into the meadow. White dog, white grass, white moonlight.

Laika didn't know how to go up steps.

"She's still learning," Mary said. "It takes a while. Go up ahead of her and call her. She'll follow."

I did what Mary suggested. I stood on the flat part of the deck and called Laika. She put her front paws up on the steps, looked around, then trotted off. Sebastian came instead. He put his gigantic head against my leg. I scruffed his neck, then called Laika again.

She came to the bottom of the steps. She appeared puzzled. Mary said maybe the fact that the stairs had no back to them might be making her more nervous. The best place to teach dogs to climb stairs, Mary said, was on big cement ones in public places. Then they would hardly see the difference between the regular ground and the risers.

"Here's one thing you can do," Mary said.

She reached in her pocket, waved a biscuit under Laika's nose, and put the biscuit on the second step. Sebastian made a move for it, but Fred clucked and the big dog sat down. Laika put her paws up again. This time she seemed more serious about it. Mary slowly placed another biscuit on the third step. Laika's rear end started jiggling.

"Go ahead, Laika," Mary said.

Fred told me to squat. "If you lower your body posture," he said, "dogs see you as less of a threat and are more willing to approach."

I squatted.

Laika jumped and put her hind legs on the first step, lifted her front legs to the second step. Reward. She gobbled the biscuit. The next biscuit waited just above her. She put her paws up again. Repeated the process.

"Smart little thing," Mary said.

I don't know why, but I was crying.

•

My mother kept a lizard in an aquarium on the kitchen table. A boyfriend had given him to her. The boyfriend left but the lizard stayed. We named the lizard Mumps because he had fat cheeks. You wouldn't think you could like a lizard very much, but I liked Mumps. So did Mom. We built him an environment and watched him climb up sticks and so on. He ate dead flies. Sometimes he ate a little hamburger meat. Mumps died when my mom took a long vacation and put me over at Killy's house. Killy was her friend and she took care of me sometimes. I told Killy that we needed to go feed Mumps, but she just kept smoking cigarettes. Killy watched a lot of TV. I knew Mumps would be dead by the time anyone remembered him. And I guess he was, but I never saw him. The aquarium was gone when I went back to live with Mom. When I asked her where Mumps had gone, she said she sold him to a pet store. She needed the money, she said. She was sorry. But really, I think, Mumps died on our kitchen table.

4

Bobby watched a lot of kung-fu movies and he told me you can lighten your tread if you walk just so. You have to think that your body is lighter. You have to imagine yourself as air. He used to lay paper bags or newspapers down on the ground. Then he'd try to walk without making a sound. He was serious about it, too. He practiced his Tai Chi moves as he walked, pretending he fought off a whole squadron of ninjas. Back and forth. Silent.

It sounds crazy, I know, but I tried to imitate Bobby when I left my room. I didn't know how late it was, but I knew the Potters were asleep. The phone—the only phone I saw—was one of those wall things. The Potters didn't like many modern things, and the phone was anything but modern. You had to stand in the kitchen to use it.

I prayed Bobby's cell worked.

The house creaked. I don't care if you *were* a ninja, the house creaked.

Sebastian lifted his head when I made it to the woodstove. I had a terrifying moment wondering what would happen if he mistook me for a burglar. He looked at me, then put his head down. I whispered, "Good boy" to him, then crept by.

Mary was one of those women who cleaned the whole kitchen before she went to bed. I'd seen her do it. Now I was grateful because I could find the phone without worrying about kicking over a pot or anything. I picked up the phone. I dialed Bobby.

He was high.

I could tell as soon as he spoke. He was way high.

"Baby," he nearly shouted, "where are you?"

"New Hampshire," I whispered.

He laughed a long, silly laugh.

"Where are you?" I asked.

"Paulie's. We scored some big tooties. We're kicking."

"Come get me," I said.

"Where the hell are you?"

"In New Hampshire," I said. "I told you."

Somebody yelled in the background. Maybe Paulie. Then I heard some cans fall. Even though I knew the Potters couldn't hear what was going on the other end of the line, I made a *shhhhh* sound anyway.

"Sorry, Baby," Bobby said. "It's mucked up around here."

"Come get me."

"Where in New Hampshire? Freaking New Hampshire?"

"Cow-freaking Hampshire, Bobby. Listen to me. I'm living with some foster parents named Potter. It's northern New Hampshire somewhere."

"I'll find you," he said.

"You better," I said.

"We're sleeping inside tonight. That's what the big deal is."

"At Paulie's?"

"No, at Ginger's. She's leaving the garage open. We're crashing in her old man's Cherokee."

"Decent," I said.

Something else fell. Then someone whooped.

"I have to go," I said.

"I'll find you," he said. "Potter. Hey, Paulie, remember the name Potter."

Someone laughed.

"He's fried," Bobby said.

"I have to go. I love you."

"I'm so gone."

"I know," I said. "It's okay."

I slipped Laika out of her crate. She didn't make any noise. I lifted her and held her close to my chest. Then I tiptoed. I carried her back to my bed and tucked her low against my belly. She was long enough to reach up and lick my face. I held her hand. Her paw. Soon she snored in tiny puppy snores. I kissed the top of her head. I thought of Mumps, and I thought of Bobby. Bobby seemed far away, like starlight, like summer.

I heard the sound of buckets. I heard the metal hasp drop against the metal body. Then I heard barking. I couldn't tell for certain what time it was, but I knew it had to be early. The light coming through the window stretched across the room like a soft, gray broom.

Next I heard growling. And for a lazy moment it seemed to be part of the outside sounds. It came closer and closer or I grew more awake, and then I understood that Laika had the edge of the comforter and was busy shaking it back and forth.

"No," I said.

She growled more and shook the comforter harder.

I smelled urine.

"Gross," I said, and climbed out.

I saw the wet spot next to my outline in the bed. "Jesus Christ!" I said.

I grabbed Laika and carried her out to the crate. Mary stood in the kitchen, cooking. She turned and looked at me.

"I wondered where she got to," she said.

She looked calm. A hippie chick with a gray ponytail.

"She peed in the bed," I said. "Right in the bed."

"If you take her out of the crate at night, she's likely to do that. Here are some paper towels. And a cleanser. Pull off the sheet and we'll change it, but scrub the mattress."

She put a roll of Scott paper towels on the kitchen counter. Then she plunked a bottle of orange cleanser next to it. I grabbed it and headed back.

"Baby?" she asked.

I turned.

"How was Bobby?" she asked.

I kept the shower hot. I felt the water sting the imprint of the tiger on my butt. Looking in the mirror, the tiger seemed all scabs. It felt annoying more than anything else. I wondered what the big appeal of tattoos was.

I put on a pair of jeans Mary had bought me. And a thick sweater. I didn't care if they thought it was a sign of giving in to them. I knew it wasn't, and that was enough. I didn't like Mary's little comment about Bobby. Was I supposed to think she had miraculous powers because she figured out I called Bobby? Why didn't she just say she heard me?

When I stepped out in the main room, Mary asked me to take Laika out to her cage. I ignored her. I sat next to the woodstove and didn't do anything. After a while, I picked up a magazine and looked at it. Screw them. The magazine had good comics. Other than that, it blew.

I figured Bobby, the way he thinks, would go about it this way: First, he would try 411. Potters in New Hampshire. He would score a map somewhere and call towns. Potters in Franconia. Potters in Piermont. Eventually he would get a list of names. The only thing working against him, as I saw it, was that Potter was a fairly common name. He might have trouble sorting out which Potter he needed. He was tricky that way, though. He could figure out a ruse to get the information he needed. He might call and say he had a delivery for a Ginny Schultz, my real name, and wait and see what happens. If Mary or Fred answered the phone, Bobby would be able to hear the pause in their voices. Then he'd know where I was.

Second, he would steal a car. Or he would borrow one. He'd drive all night to get up here and he'd figure out a way to let me know he's waiting. If he does that, we'll be gone before they know it. And this time we'll be gone for good. I'll tell him that. I'll tell him this time we won't hang around the old spots. We have to go. We have to clear out. We'll go west, or maybe down to Mexico. I've never been to Mexico and neither has Bobby.

"We got four inches last night," Mary said. "It's good snow."

I didn't say anything.

Mary sat on the couch, not far from me. I didn't put down the magazine.

"Fred is hooking up the dogs. He thought you might want to go for a ride."

I didn't say anything.

She stood and went back to the kitchen.

Laika began whining. At first I didn't give a damn. But she needed to go out, I could tell, and Mary was playing her game of guiding me by silence. Again, big lesson. I was supposed to take care of Laika.

I was bored anyway, so I put down the magazine, put on one of their heavy jackets, stepped into some muck boots, and let Laika out of the cage. Almost before she took a step she started to lower her butt to pee, so I scooped her up and hustled her outside. I put her down on the deck. When I looked up, the world had changed.

Snow covered everything. It pressed the lowest limbs of the pines down into the ground, and the meadow had turned brilliant white. The air had changed, too, and now it smelled rich and cold, like something you had to collect as much as breathe. It made me happy to see the snow and to feel the air charged with new energy. Laika seemed to sense it, too, because she nearly dove off the deck.

We followed Fred's tracks to the dog yard.

"Good morning," he said. "Did you come down for a ride?"

"Sure," I said, for the hell of it.

"Well, I'm finished hydrating them. You have to water them about an hour before you run a team. My younger team is ready. I'll run the older team when we get back."

"Where do you run them?"

He waved out. Out into the woods. Out on the land. "I built a circle. It goes about seven miles. In and out, round about. The sprint races we run are about six miles, so this is good training. We'll take that rig there."

He pointed at a metal three-wheeled contraption. It looked like a motorcycle, only wider and heavier. It had no engine—the dogs served as the engine, I guessed—but it looked sturdy enough. Maybe you would call it a chariot made of pipes. In any case, he had a line attached to it already.

"Why don't you put Laika in the cage there? Then we can start to line out. Mary should be along to help."

I told Laika she was a little stinker when I put her in the cage. But I also gave her a kiss. I went back to where Fred stood next to the chariot thing.

"We call this a rig. Most people have it for dry-land training. Once the snow comes, you use sleds, of course. But right now we still have to ride on this. A neighbor of mine packs the trail down with his snowmobile. Eventually it will be a track."

I nodded.

The dogs behind me had gone zoo-y. They wanted to run.

Mary came across the meadow. She had a wool hat on over her gray hair. She looked pretty in a mom sort of way. Fred waved to her. He was big but excited as a boy. "Isn't this snow pretty?" he shouted.

"It's beautiful!" she said.

He said to me, "Do me a favor, will you? I want you to hold out the gangline."

"What's that?" I asked.

He waved for me to follow. He picked up the line at the very front. He handed it to me.

"When we hook up the dogs," he nearly yelled, because the dogs had gone nuts now that they saw us getting ready, "they'll pull and fuss. Just keep the line taut. You'll see."

I grabbed the line. I didn't have any gloves.

Fred moved pretty fast. And Mary arrived in time to help him. Fred reached one hand into a dog run and pulled out a dog. I had no idea which dog it was, but it looked lean and flat-chested. Fred held the dog's front legs off the ground and walked the dog to a spot a few feet away from me. Then he hooked the dog in place. Neckline, backline. The dog started yanking like crazy against the gangline.

Mary and Fred worked together. You could tell they wanted to hustle, but they worked in rhythm. Mary walked a dog up to me and hooked it right next to my hands.

"Charlie," she shouted. "A leader."

They hooked up six dogs. Three pairs along the line as it led back to the sled. I couldn't believe the energy the dogs put into the line. It felt like it wanted to vibrate. It wasn't only the strength of the animals but their desire to go. They wanted to run, to be anywhere out in the snow, to take off. I liked that about them.

"Do you have a hat?" Mary shouted when they were all lined out.

I shook my head.

"Here," she said and plucked her hat off. She handed it to me. She slipped off her gloves and handed them to me, too. I tried not to take them, but it was cold and I was going and she was staying back. It made sense.

"Climb on," she said.

I had to climb into a small part directly in front of where the driver stood. Mary ducked back into the dog yard and came out with a blanket. She threw it over my legs. I felt Fred step onto the back of the rig. You couldn't help but feel his strength. I started to laugh, because I suddenly pictured Bobby and his nitwits watching me riding on a rig. I couldn't wait to tell them. They would think I'd gone completely nuts.

"As you love me," Fred shouted.

I had no idea what he meant by that.

Then he lifted something or released a brake, and we took off.

5

Silence.

After all that barking, silence.

I'm not sure why, but the first thing I saw, truly saw, were the flecks of snow coming up from underneath the dogs' paws. They flew up like protons. I kept watching them, thinking: the dogs are the present, and the flecks of snow coming up are already the past.

It was not like the movies. It was not complicated and grand. Not in a movie way. The dogs ran quietly, all business, their tongues out of the side of their mouths. The rig made no noise, and Fred did not speak. The sun had warmed enough so that it shoveled snow off some of the pine boughs, and here and there we saw tiny avalanches. But you couldn't see anything without knowing that the dogs gave you this vision, that they took you and carried you and did not expect one thing in return.

I thought of my mother. I thought of one time when we went to a plant nursery. She had this idea to make our small apartment look better by putting plants around it. The nursery had big wagons that you filled with plants as you went. Then you wheeled it to the checkout. My mother put me in the wagon and pulled me around the nursery grounds. She loved to shop and she had enough money that particular day and she was in a happy mood. She kept handing me more plants and soon I hardly had room in the wagon. People stopped and pointed at us, and my mom ate up the attention. I knew she was happy and that made me happy. I remember her walking up ahead, and sometimes she pretended to be a pony and other times she pretended to be *Mathahahttahhhahah* the elephant. She made the name sound funny when she pronounced it.

When we paid for the plants, the plant lady pretended I was another plant. She looked at me and said she wasn't sure what kind of plant I was so she didn't know what to charge my mom. Then I chirped up and said, "I'm not a plant." It was not such a funny line—even I knew it wasn't that funny—but my mom laughed and the lady laughed and I was happy to be the cause of it.

"On by," Fred said. That meant "keep going."

Way up front, Charlie kept the team lined out. I didn't know the name of the other leader. But they ran in a fast dog run, both of them joined by necklines. The slightly bigger dogs closer to us supplied the main pull. Fred told me that. The dogs closest to us were called wheel dogs. The middle dogs ran point. The leaders were leaders, and their job was to run as fast as they could. Fred said no team runs faster than its leader. That just made sense. Fred said a top sprint team runs nearly thirty miles an hour. Being a leader is exhausting because the dog has to run faster than all the other dogs, and it has to make correct choices. When people win the Iditarod—the famous race in Alaska—and they thank their leaders,

Fred said, they meant it. It wasn't just talk. Leaders won races, not people really. Fred said Laika probably had what it took to be a leader. She had good bloodlines.

I kept thinking: this is what I want to remember about sitting in a dog rig.

But things moved fast, too fast, and as soon as I latched on to one idea, something pulled me to the next. Pines, tons of pines. The trail went up for a few minutes, then it arched down, to the left, and we glided. I worried that we would run up on the dogs, but Fred touched the brake—a metal pedal that dug into the snow. It made a sound like an ice skate carving a turn at high speed.

At the bottom of the hill, a red-tailed squirrel ran past us. Fred told me later it was a red-tailed squirrel, because I couldn't say for sure what it was. But it squirted past and suddenly the dogs—each one in line—flicked its ears forward. I had thought they had been all business before, but the squirrel got them moving like crazy. They wanted that squirrel. Fred yelled, "On by, Charlie," but she wanted that squirrel, too. We squeezed over to the right side of the track and suddenly the trees flashed by too close. Fred cursed quickly under his breath, and the right wheel of the rig went up. We hung like the top of a trap waiting to fall, balanced on two wheels, and I thought we couldn't miss a patch of birches in front of us. I put out both hands on the bars to steady myself and thought about jumping, but then we hit a rock or something on the other side from where we were leaning and it snapped us back onto our wheels. Fred shouted, "Haw," meaning left, and Charlie finally listened. She danced back over, the other lead dog running with her, and then the team moved like a furry snake to follow her path. The squirrel had long ago disappeared and now we flopped back onto the trail. Trees arched above us, oaks, and we shot down the tunnel of them like a bullet following the sides of a gun barrel.

"What did you think?" Mary asked.

We sat by the woodstove and drank hot chocolate. Sebastian sat at my feet and watched me. His eyes followed my hand from the cup to my lips. He did not drool or try to come closer for a handout. His chest spread as wide as my hips.

"I like it," I said. "It was better than I thought it would be."

"I'm glad," Mary said. "We'll be racing, you know. Most weekends."

"Where do you race?"

"Different spots. Sometimes in towns. Sometimes on lakes. Over in Vermont and in Maine, too."

"I'm not allowed to leave the state," I said.

"We okayed it with Cindy."

"You just race all weekend?"

"Usually they have a dinner afterward. Once in a while they have speakers—dog people, mostly. You know. Vets, or other mushers. They have tips and some videos."

She looked at me. "I guess that sounds kind of dull to you," she said.

"I like the dogs," I said.

"You could run a sled," she said. "Race, if you want to. We have almost a month to practice. If you like, you can take them out three or four times a week to learn and get the feel . . ."

"I would drive the sled?" I asked.

"Yes," she said. "With the dogs."

I felt my heart lift a little. I couldn't quite figure what it would mean to run a sled. I mean, I knew what the words meant, but I didn't know what the information was doing down in my chest. I knew it was part of their therapy to put me in charge of dogs, get me to see things cooperatively, and all that junk. But the dogs didn't know that.

I didn't answer. I saw the reflection of my face in the glimmer of the chocolate. It was just a silhouette, but I could make out my nose stud.

"Just before Fred ran," I said, "he shouted something. What did he say?"

She thought for a minute. Then she smiled. "He shouts, 'As you love me' before he runs. Fred's a sentimentalist. It comes from passage in *Call of the Wild.* Do you know the book?"

I shook my head. I had heard of the title, or maybe saw the movie, but I liked sitting there listening to her talk. I put a hand on Sebastian's head. His fur felt as thick as scrub brush.

"This fellow—John, I think his name is—has this great dog named Buck. And John makes a bet in a barroom that Buck can pull a ton or something. Some extravagant weight. No dog can do it, of course, but John takes the bet. And when he gets his Buck all harnessed and the crowd gathers around, John kneels next to Buck and whispers in his ear, 'As you love me.' Fred always gets teary-eyed when he reads it and, believe me, he reads it at the start of every dog-sledding season."

"And does he?" I asked.

"Read it?"

"No, does Buck pull the sled?"

"Do you want me to tell you, or do you want to read the book?"

"Tell me."

"Well, it turns out," Mary said, "that the sled had sat out all night, or something, I don't remember, and the runners had frozen. So when John wanted to break the runners free, the fellow who held his bet said no, that was part of the deal. Buck had to pull the sled, but first he had to break out the runners."

"How would he do that?"

"John told him to go gee, then haw, then gee again. And the sled broke free. Then Buck lowered his stance and put his shoulders into it and the sled moved forward an inch. Then another inch. Then one more. And finally it was moving."

"So John won the bet?"

Mary nodded.

And she said, "And Fred, the old cornball, yells it out before he runs. Kid him if he forgets. Ask him if the dogs ran only as though they sort of liked him."

I looked at Sebastian. I realized I had never seen him blink.

I dialed Bobby. I dialed at two o'clock when Mary took a nap and Fred went to town. Bobby's phone reported that he had no service. I knew that could mean almost anything. He could be traveling. He could have turned it off. He could be arrested. Almost anything.

I dialed him again five minutes later. Still no service.

I put my hand down the back of my jeans and fingered the tiger tattoo. It hurt. It felt like Wan had slipped a tiger under my skin. For a second I worried it had become infected. I felt with my fingers to see if it had swollen more since the morning. But I couldn't tell anything definite.

I dialed Bobby again. No service.

I wondered why girls wait. Girls always wait for boys.

I did a page of math problems. Algebra. They were dumb. Mary looked them over after I finished. She said she didn't care if I got them correct. She just wanted to make sure I was trying.

Her glasses reflected light. Biofocals. They reflected light every time she bent her head. The math appeared reversed in her glasses. Watching her, I pretended I was Chinese and this was my math teacher and somewhere I would smell orange blossoms.

At sunset I took Laika out. She flew out of the kennel when I opened the door and she ran in a nutty circle around me. Snow flew up from under her feet. She looked incredibly white against the snow. She could lie down in the meadow and you wouldn't see her.

I got down on my knees and let her charge up to me. Then she wrestled a little, lifting her paws the way boxers lift their hands. She had sharp little puppy teeth and once she bit at my glove and I told her to leave it alone.

Fred came down and showed me how to harness a dog. We harnessed Laika four or five times before I got the hang of it. It isn't easy. You have to push the harness over their heads, then swing it around under their bellies. Laika didn't like sitting still for it. When we had her in harness, we tied a small log to a rope and attached it to the tail ring at the back of the harness.

"Go ahead and run in front of her," Fred told me.

I did.

Laika didn't like having something dragging along behind her. Not at first. She kept sitting and turning around. She couldn't quite figure what it meant, this thing behind her. But then she ran a little more confidently. Then a little more. Fred started feeding dogs while I ran Laika in a large circle.

"You can unhook her," Fred said when I returned.

"Do all sled dogs know how to pull?"

"Hard to say," Fred said.

He filled each bowl with food. Then he poured hot water on it. The food steamed and the dogs ate it in fast, greedy gulps when he set it before them.

Fred said, "It's the old nurture versus nature argument. Are dogs genetically disposed to pull? Or do we teach them to? You can teach almost any dog to pull, but sled dogs do it better."

"Why?"

"It's their pace, for one thing. It's tricky to run while you're pulling things. In theory, a greyhound should be the best dog for a sled, but they leave the ground when they run. So for a second they are suspended. Sled dogs always have a foot on the ground. At least that's what I've read."

"You people are nuts up here," I said.

Fred turned and smiled. He's a nice man. He's like Sebastian.

After we finished feeding the dogs, I walked Laika on a leash to teach her some manners. She pulled and yanked at the leash, so we had to work on that. She had to understand that pulling a sled is one thing, but it's another thing to pull on the leash. It's probably complicated for a dog.

Fred went back to the house, and I had a nice moment with Laika. She was tired from running around and pulling things. I picked her up and held her on my lap. She's a little big for that, but I found a bench near the kennels and hoisted her over my knees. She didn't curl up or anything. She just sat on my lap, her head at about my level. We looked at the sun going behind the trees. I thought about how much my mom would have liked Laika. It seemed like my mom never had time to like anything too much. When she did, it disappeared. Like Mumps. Like some of the men she liked so much.

I put my chin over Laika's head and let her direct my gaze wherever she liked. We followed the track of the sun and a few birds that ended the day in the branches of a pine. For an instant, I could hardly tell the difference between Laika and me. We watched the world like dogs watch the world. And that was okay.

6

We woke early the day of the first race. The thermometer read six degrees. Fred pulled a large red Ford F-250 around to the back of the house. The truck had dog boxes on top. Dog boxes are these things that house the dogs when you travel. To get the dogs in, you have to lift them or point them up and they jump. Then you close them inside and they snuggle down in the straw. Not hay, straw. Hay takes on moisture. Straw doesn't.

It was ridiculously early, though.

The sun had just cleared the mountain behind the house. But I liked working with the dogs. I admit it. I had been with them three and a half weeks and I had worked with the dogs every day. I knew the foster care people had put me with the Potters because of the dogs—the dogs helping to center me, is how they would put it—but I didn't care. The dogs didn't know anything about my past, or about the plans Cindy had made for my rehabilitation, or about anything much except that day, that minute, that feeding. I liked that.

I helped Fred load the dogs. We loaded the dogs in pairs, two to a box. The dogs barked like nuts. They wanted to go. Racing was what they lived for, Fred said. When we had them all in, we opened the side doors and let Sebastian in the rear of the cab. Then we lashed two sleds on top of the truck. We stored buckets of food and water in the back of the dog box. Harnesses. Bowls. And extra hooks, snaps, you name it.

Laika came out last. I put her in a box with Muppin. When I put my fingers to the hole of her individual box, she licked to say hello.

"Like Noah's ark," Fred said when we climbed in and pulled back around to pick up Mary.

I had been spending a lot of time with Fred, and I have to say I had never met a man like him. He was wicked smart, but he never showed off. He liked to do chores, and he liked the dogs. But most guys do stuff just so women will watch them. Fred didn't. He didn't really care what anyone thought of him. He wore nice clothes, always clean, but they were never fancy. He never raised his voice. Now and then people called from New York—old clients, he said—and you could tell he was interested but that that part of his life had gone by. He reminded me of those candies that have a hard outside and a mushy part inside. He came from Wisconsin originally. He grew up on a farm.

And the other thing about Fred is this: I never felt like a woman around him. I never had to worry about all that stuff. Never had to think, well, I'm a girl, he's a guy, and so on. None of that. I know it sounds weird to even talk about it, but that's the truth.

We picked up Mary at the front door. She had a picnic basket full of food. Coffee thermos, muffins, juice. Sometimes she gets carried away a little with all the touches—the Martha Stewart stuff—but you always like the food. I sat in back with Sebastian. He sniffed at the picnic basket.

"Nicky called," Mary said as she finally climbed in.

Nicky was their son.

"He'll meet us at the race," she said. "He has to go back tonight, but he wanted to see the dogs."

"Does Nicky race?" I asked.

"He's a great musher," Fred said. "But he's a resident at Dartmouth-Hitchcock, the hospital in Hanover. He doesn't have much spare time."

"Sebastian belongs to Nicky," Mary said. "They were cubs together."

Humans did not domesticate dogs.

Think about it. It doesn't make sense. Why would a primitive man or woman stop their hunting and gathering in order to bring a food-consuming creature closer? No, dogs domesticated themselves. That's what I read in a book that was in the backseat of the truck. This author went to villages around the world and looked at dump dogs. Dogs that hung out at dumps. And what he discovered is that dogs always hung around human habitations. And little by little, dogs approached humans. We may have let them in the door, but they knew enough to knock.

This author also talked about flight response. Wolves have a flight response that is more hair-trigger than a dog's flight response. In other words, if you approach a wolf feeding at a dump, the wolf flees immediately and doesn't return for a long time. A dog, on the other hand, waits longer to run (and gets a last gobble or two) and then returns more quickly. Flight response is a big deal in this book. The farther you run away from something, the longer it takes to return, the more difficult your chances of survival.

That's this guy's point, anyway.

I thought of my mother. Everyone had a flight response. Some people have to run pretty far away from pain or a bad turn. Bobby's flight response is like a dog's. He gets past things quickly, though he remembers the cause of the pain. But my mom, she's a wolf. She scatters as soon as something threatens. And it takes her a long time to return.

And Fred and Mary, they're already domesticated. They don't have to scatter, because they belong. They stay right at the dump and get a belly full. Nothing scares them away.

We drove into Vermont. The Connecticut River looked like a white tape someone used to join New Hampshire to Vermont.

You could hear the dogs even before you saw the race site. We cut down three or four dirt roads, the surfaces tucked with snow and ice, and then we rounded a red barn and saw the racers. Probably fifty trucks stood in rows on a cornfield. The whole thing looked a little crazy and a little exciting. I could imagine what Bobby would say if he could see a couple hundred people, and maybe a thousand dogs, lined up in a cornfield on a Saturday morning in six-degree weather.

Fred slowed the truck and talked to a fellow who wore a hat with a fur lining.

"Over there," the man said, and pointed to a parking spot.

We chucked over the uneven ground and parked between two other trucks. Our dogs began barking. And the dogs in the other trucks barked back. Sebastian sat up and looked out the window. He didn't bark. He didn't have to.

•

In six-degree weather you can't feel your fingers, your toes, your cheeks. If you tear, your eyes get icy. Your touch becomes clumsy. In six-degree weather snow creaks like wood when you walk over it.

We suspended a chain from the front of the truck to the rear. Every two feet along the length, another chain came out to hold a dog. The dogs could move and eat and drink, but they couldn't get into mischief.

We dropped dogs. Dropping dogs means you let them out of the truck to do what they need to do. Then you scoop it up. My job was to scoop. Fred lifted down the dogs. Mary went to register for the race. We dropped only one team—Muppin, Charlie, Teddy Roosevelt, Second Boss, Rocky, and Willow. Fred said we had to be ready to run pretty soon. I helped him lift down the sled. He rigged up the gangline. Then he let Sebastian out and attached him to a line.

I looked around. Everywhere people dropped dogs out of boxes. Some dogs already sat calmly, waiting. A tent with hot dogs and coffee for sale took up one end of the cornfield. Some Port-a-Johns.

"They're going to have a mushers' meeting in ten minutes," Mary said when she came back. "Baby, here's your number."

She handed me number 33.

Greg, president of the New England Sled Dog Club, held up a map of the course. He stood on an overturned bucket. He shouted so everyone could hear. He wore a bright orange vest that declared him the race official. "The course is running fine. We groomed it last night and again this morning," he said, pointing as he spoke. "You should have no problem with any of the turns. There is a good downhill on this bend, and a bit of a slowdown here. Just take it easy through this section. We have helpers out on the trail, so if you have difficulty, we'll come to the rescue."

People laughed.

"We're going to start with the six-dog teams. We will begin at eight ten. Everyone ready?"

People laughed and shouted again.

"There's a spaghetti dinner tonight at seven o'clock. Please attend if you can. It's in the Wells River Junior High. Proceeds go to the club, of course. So, good luck. I need plenty of help at the starting line and with the flags. Pitch in and we'll have a good day."

Mary walked back with me. Fred went to get a cup of coffee.

"You're running first," she said. "You've practiced everything. You should be all set. Think you can do it?"

I nodded.

She put her arm around me. Squeezed my shoulders.

Nicky showed up as we harnessed the team.

He was the most handsome man I had ever seen. He resembled Brad Pitt. People say that sometimes about guys, but it was genuine with Nicky. You could see girls, even moms, looking at him when he walked among the dog trucks.

"This is Baby," Fred said while harnessing dogs. "Glad you're here. Baby, Nicky."

I shook hands with him. He stood three inches taller than I did, and he wore an Inca-style wool hat. I couldn't speak.

Mary hugged Nicky.

"Baby's running the team," Mary said. "She's been practicing. She's got the hang of it."

"So I heard," Nicky said and looked at me.

I had to look away.

Then Nicky saw Sebastian. Sebastian saw him, too, and began to bark. Sebastian rarely barked.

"There's my boy," Nicky said.

He went over to the truck, and Sebastian mauled him. They smooched and stayed close together, almost like they needed to whisper something to each other. The other dogs gave them room. It was a little uncanny to watch.

"How do you like my boy?" Mary asked me, grinning, because she obviously knew how drop-dead gorgeous he was.

I just looked at her.

Then Cindy showed up.

I didn't even know it was Cindy until she got up close. She wore about a thousand pounds of clothes, and she had her lover lesbo partner with her. You could tell they were lesbians because they both looked like guys with bad haircuts. Bobby would have made fun of them. They would have cracked him up.

"How are you?" Cindy asked. "Baby, this is my friend, Catie."

They stood in front of me. It was six degrees. Nicky, the beautiful, had returned from the truck. Fred harnessed dogs like a madman, and Mary just watched it all. In a way, it was funny. Cindy's visit was so ridiculously transparent. She was the good social worker following through, supporting me, and that might not have been bad except she brought her partner along. That way it could be a date, sort of, and at the same time she could show off how socially caring she was, and then they could go back and make out and tell each other how sensitive they were. It bothered me. I didn't mind Nicky because he knew dogs. But Cindy didn't. And Catie appeared frightened of all the noise and animals.

I didn't have time to think. Mary looked at the starting line.

"Three ahead of you," she shouted over the barking. "It's time."

If you've never driven a dog team, this is how you do it.

You stand on the runners. You never say "Mush." You hold onto the handle and you lean with the dogs when they take a turn. Most of the time you watch them, watch the line so it doesn't go slack and snap you on a turn, and you pump. You pump like you would on a scooter. You kick and pump and you glide along. If you do it right, the pumping augments the momentum of the sled but doesn't overwhelm it. You don't want to shove it up next to your dogs. Harmony. Balance. All that.

Good dogs do not quit. They run until their hearts give out. They run until their feet leave rosebuds of blood on the snow.

Nothing you do can repay what the dogs do for you.

"Five ... , four ... , three ... , two ... , one ... , go, driver!"

That's what they say to start you.

I know they say it because I heard them start other drivers, but I didn't hear it when they counted me down. Suddenly Fred and Nicky and Mary—who had been holding the sled an instant before—stepped back and lifted away. I saw Charlie snap into her harness, then Willow, and suddenly the sled moved under me. Fast. The handlebar jerked my arms and nearly pulled me straight out, like a limp piece of laundry, and we were off.

"As you love me," I whispered.

But that was the last thought I had. My brain shrunk down, and it became quiet and solid and as calm as it had ever been. I liked running dogs and I had practiced enough and I knew what I was doing. I squatted down, as Fred had showed me, and dangled behind the handlebar to reduce wind resistance. Then I felt Charlie begin to turn, and I could see the wheel dogs, the big males, dig in to pivot, and I popped up and began to pump. We spun down, down, to the left, and the trees zipped by and I glided and it was just dogs and snow. "Gee over, gee over," I shouted to get them moving right, and we slid around the first turn. I had a hard time knowing what my speed was relative to the other teams, but I caught a team in front of me and yelled, "Trail!"

The driver pulled over and braked his dogs and I yelled, "On by, Charlie, on by!" And we did. No fuss. No fight. *Damn it, damn it, damn it, you're beautiful*, that's all I could think. All I could think. *You're beautiful, beautiful. Run.*

Second Boss nearly stumbled but caught himself and we kept going.

We banked up and then down, took a belly flop, where you're suspended for just a second and then the ground is under you again. A trail helper shouted that I was flying and I yelled something, thanks something, but frost had started to coat my eyes. My hands disappeared and I might have been holding the sled with my wrists. I hoped the dogs knew what they were doing.

"Oh, Charlie, Charlie, Charlie," I chanted.

Then we took the downhill. It was huge. The sled started to slip down on the wheel dogs and I shouted to them to move faster. I didn't want to touch the brake. I wanted go faster, and we did. The sled shot down the hill, and I tried to remember if we had a turn at the bottom. But then I forgot everything, trusted the dogs, sang something deep in me, the Charlie chant, the song to Willow. *Run, babies, run. Run, Baby.*

We skidded on the downhill turn, but I cornered okay. I'm not sure how. Then the woods dropped away and we skidded out onto the lake. I hadn't even known there *was* a lake, but we were on it, *pow,* and one other team came into sight. My dogs saw the team, too, and nothing, nothing, could stop them from flying after them. I saw Muppin's ears go back and I dropped behind the sled, hung like a monkey to let them go. When they slowed a little, I braked, as Fred had told me to—to give them a breather—then shouted to get going. The change of pace can crank them up, and it did. I had done it right, and the dogs charged, their paws flooding the air with pellets of snow and ice. I pumped behind them, matching my push to their speed, relieving them of weight for a second.

The sun scratched a hole through the trees as we rounded the farthest bend and started back. It fell ahead of us, pointing, and for a curious second I felt the dogs did not run with the sled but ran tethered to my heart. I began to cry, I'm not sure why, I just did, and they were so beautiful, so willing, and they trusted me.

"Bring us home, bring us home!" I shouted.

We passed the second team in the final half mile. I yelled, "Trail!" By rule, he did not have to yield in this last stretch, but he did. He slipped over and my team passed his, the second of the run, and I saw the finish line. I knew it had been a good run. I knew it had been a good run, a fantastic run, and I pumped hard to get them in. "On by, Charlie!" I yelled as we came into the finish chute. I saw the president's orange vest, and I saw Fred, sweet Fred, waiting ready to catch the team. Nicky stood beside him, and I let the dogs run into their hands. They grabbed Willow and Charlie and trotted us back to the truck, where Cindy and her friend waited. I jumped off the sled as soon as it was safe and fell on my knees beside Muppin and put my face in his frosted fur and didn't look up for a long time. I heard his breath going through his lungs and felt his knees quivering with the whole trail stored in the muscles of his legs.

7

Nicky told me this story:

Long ago, the Empress of China loved small dogs. She bred Pekinese, the smaller the better. Her kennel consisted of bamboo cages lined up along one corridor of her palace. She charged her eunuchs with the responsibility of caring for the dogs. They did so gladly and with great skill. Still, the Empress toured the kennels when she liked and often culled the biggest dogs. She ordered that the large, clumsy dogs be slaughtered. The eunuchs, who had grown to love the dogs, could not bring themselves to murder the dogs. Risking their lives, they passed the dogs to friends and family members and asked them to transport the dogs far away.

Had the eunuchs not disobeyed the Empress, the Pekinese breed would have disappeared altogether. As it turned out, invaders entered the palace in the next year and killed all the servants. They also killed the Empress and her dogs. Only the imperfect dogs—ones that had been given away—survived.

For some years, people believed only female dogs had escaped. A worldwide search went out for a male. Surely, people said, one male dog lived. For years the dogs' owners believed the breed was doomed. Then one day by chance, a woman with a female Pekinese walked down a New York street and came across a male. The owner

"I do, actually," he said.

I pulled out a cigarette anyway and lit it.

I blew the smoke straight ahead.

"Is that supposed to be cool?" he asked. "Are you showing off?"

I didn't say anything.

Here's the thing: I have this problem where I see what I'm doing, know I shouldn't do it, and do it anyway. Like with Nicky. I had no reason to be a jackass to him. But I wanted to be. I don't know why.

Maybe he was too handsome.

Maybe it was the swing music and the nice truck.

I like things falling apart, though. That's my thing. Because when everything else is chaotic, my problems seem less important or less out of the ordinary. Counselors always tell me that. Cindy even told me that.

With Nicky I waited for him to explode. His behavior and mine existed on a scale that didn't mean very much—the difference didn't mean very much. If I could get him angry, I guess, we would be even. I finished the cigarette and threw it out the window. He didn't talk the rest of the way.

I finished second when they posted the results of the day's heat.

On Sunday we had to race again, but I was in second place in the six-dog sportsman division. Greg, the president, had posted the starting times for the next day. He stood beside an easel with the printout of today's race results. His face looked tired from the cold.

Cindy found me right after they posted the times. She carried a big plate of spaghetti. She smiled at me and nodded that we should sit. Everyone else still waited in line. This was *our time,* I knew. She wanted to go over things. It was pathetic.

"So you finished second," Cindy said. "That's just terrific."

"Is that your girlfriend?" I asked.

"Catie? Yes, why?"

"I wondered, that's all. I didn't know."

"Didn't know what?"

"That you were a lesbo."

"I'm bisexual."

"Give me a break."

Cindy twirled the spaghetti on the tines of the fork. She used the plate as a platter to spin against. I knew she was trying to remain calm.

"The Potters say you're doing great," she said.

I didn't say anything.

"And your work with the dogs has just been terrific. They said that."

I shrugged.

"Are you doing some schoolwork?"

I shrugged.

"Okay, so things are going fine," she said, "and you don't trust it. Is that why you're suddenly quiet?"

I looked over her shoulder.

She turned and looked for her girlfriend.

"You think I don't know the score?" Cindy asked. "You think I don't get it? I don't know you very well, but I know what you're doing. I've seen it a thousand times."

I shrugged.

She put her fork down. Bobby would call it the movie moment. She was going to give me *the talk* and she did.

She said, "Here's what you don't get. You're feeling pretty good about what you're doing here, so you are trying to upset the apple cart. The Potters like you, and you like them. And you like the dogs. But somewhere along the line, Baby, you learned not to trust good things. You're like a lot of kids in that way. You expect things to turn sour, so you make them come out that way even if they seem promising. Maybe you could learn to short-circuit that desire to screw things up. It doesn't help you, and it's unattractive. You may think it's cool, or aloof, but it's just bad mental health."

She stood.

"I'll give a good report. Don't worry," she said, picking up her plate. "Officially, you're on the right track. But I want to remind you that you're out of chances. You have no place to go, Baby. This is the last stop, okay? So when I see you getting ready to screw things up, I have to shake my head and say it's a real pity. Maybe you have to ask yourself why you do it, because I sure as hell don't know."

She walked away. Her friend Catie zoomed in to get the scoop. She bent over Cindy and had a bunch of whisper words for her. Then she slipped an arm around Cindy's shoulders and they headed off. They stopped for an instant in line to talk to Fred and Mary. Fred nodded, and Mary glanced at me. Then Fred and Mary returned to pushing their trays along the cafeteria rack. Cindy and Catie left.

It dipped below zero when we dropped dogs outside the motel. Three other musher trucks took up the other corners of the lot.

A soft snow fell, so it was pretty with the security lights and the sounds of dogs moving and people bundled in thick clothes. And inside, I knew, the heat would feel good and I could sleep in a plain double bed, watch TV, drink sodas. Mary had bought us all treats—Smartfood popcorn, and pretzels, and Dannon yogurts. Cindy had given the okay for me to stay in a room by myself. Originally, Mary had planned to stay with me, but Cindy said no. She said if I was determined to run away, I could figure out a way no matter what. One human cannot restrain another for very long. That's how she put it.

But I liked being out with Fred and the dogs. Fred lifted the dogs down and I circled the truck with a pooper scooper. Now and then I cleaned up a mess. Mostly the dogs peed. And peed. And peed. They wanted to be back in their quiet boxes, too, and push down into the straw to sleep.

I knelt in front of Laika after I finished cleaning the messes. This was her first race, even if she hadn't run. I gave her a biscuit and then brushed her. Her fur crackled under the brush. She had a ton of energy to burn, so I took her off her chain and walked her around. She danced back and forth and huffed at Sebastian. Then I patted my chest and she jumped up and put her paws on my belly. We danced like that for a minute.

"She'll be taller than you pretty soon," Fred said when I chained her up again.

"A lot taller, I think."

"You ran a fine race today," he said.

"The dogs just took me away."

He pursed his lips a little as if to say "maybe."

"Jerry Levaseur is in the lead," Fred said. "He's been running dogs for twenty years and you have him worried."

"We may not be as fast tomorrow."

"And you may be faster. We won't know until tomorrow. But you have an advantage. You go second, so your dogs will chase his. It's harder to run out front."

"They're your dogs, Fred. You trained them."

"Not when you drive them. They're yours in the race."

We loaded the dogs back in their boxes. I circled the truck again and gave them biscuits. It was cold, deep cold, but the dogs gave me kisses through the wire mesh of their box lids.

I called Bobby three times. No service.

Around midnight I called my mom's old phone number.

It was stupid. I knew she was gone. But I couldn't sleep and I felt like someone had a kite string tied to my heart and winds I didn't know anything about kept pulling them and making things move. I sat on the edge of the bed and turned down the volume on the TV. Then I pushed the phone numbers out of memory.

I heard the buzz go down the line and then suddenly someone picked up without the phone even ringing. Weird. I held my breath. A woman asked who it was. I strained to hear if it could be my mother. The woman said hello again.

"Is Mrs. Shultz there?" I asked.

"Who?" the woman asked.

"Mrs. Shultz?"

"Wrong number," the woman said and hung up.

I sat for a while on the edge of the bed, thinking about calling back. Maybe it was my mom, but I doubted it. More likely it was a friend of a friend, and they had passed the apartment down and someone had taken over the number. And people didn't give out information. You couldn't just call people like my mom and ask for someone by name because creditors always dunned them. Phones carried strangers inside. Only fools volunteered information.

I knew where that phone was, though. It was on a wall not far from the sink, and my mom sometimes talked with it clutched between her chin and shoulder. She did dishes and talked, and I used to sit at the kitchen table and watch. Sometimes I did homework or folded laundry. My favorite times—usually around Christmas—were when my mom put out a jigsaw puzzle at the kitchen table. We always made the same one, the scene of a harbor with tiny boats moored to the piers and the sun setting. We sat and did that puzzle in maybe two nights, and we always had snacks, and my mom always stayed in a good mood. It was best if there were no men around, no interruptions, no phone calls. But even if some guy did call, and if I knew he might drop by later, my mom didn't invite him right then. She called it "girl time." We painted our toenails, and one year we ordered out Chinese, but we kept coming back to the puzzle. A pelican flew across the setting sun in the picture, and that was part of the game. You had to see who could get the pelican each year, and I suppose my mom let me get it, but it seemed like I always won. I remember pressing that pelican into the sun. And I always wondered if the piece was meant to be the bird itself or just the shadow of a bird that flew a little higher and a little closer to the sun.

9

I watched Jerry Levaseur's team take off and then nodded for Fred to move the dogs up. I stood on the runners and felt the sled glide under me. Mary held the wheel dogs. Greg, the club president, inspected the sled and harnesses.

"Good to go," he said to me.

It was four degrees and snowing.

Fred held up his hand and began counting down. I heard the race organizer count over the microphone.

"Three ... , two ... , one ... , go, driver!"

"Go, go, go, go, go!" I yelled.

And I ducked down behind the sled.

A blur of people lined the chute. They had come to see the last races. I felt the dogs finding their rhythm as we ran around the first corner, fanning away. "As you love me," I whispered, and I felt the dogs flying up ahead, the snow everywhere. Cold air rammed against my cheeks and eyes, and I blinked to make sure my eyelids didn't freeze.

Way up ahead, I saw Jerry Levaseur's team. He wore a blue jacket, a fleece hood, and his team ran white dogs. I yelled for Charlie to catch them. Then I yelled to Willow. And we flew down the first hill, banking right, then left, the dogs fresh and willing. I didn't cry. I didn't do anything except keep my eyes on the jacket ahead of me, the dogs drifting like gray smoke ahead of the sled. I could do this. We could do this. Never had I wanted to do anything more than catch the team in front of me.

"Haw over!" I yelled, to get them left.

We flicked past a copse of birch trees, ones I hadn't seen the day before, and it was white trees, white snow, white dogs. On the flats I began to pump, matching my kick to the beat of the dogs, and the sled stayed a precise distance from Second Boss and Teddy Roosevelt. I did it right. I did it over and over and when we came around the next turn, I spotted Jerry Levaseur's team. We had gained on it. He glanced over his shoulder and I couldn't help from yelling at the top of my lungs, "Go, Charlie, go, Willow, go go go go!"

I felt crazy. I felt like maybe a dog feels on a hunt, because that was it. Here we were, everything in front of us. The dogs flattened, and I saw the huge prints of Second Boss throwing up snow, and I opened my nostrils. I breathed every breath hard and quick through my nose, and my hands ached from the cold, and my toes felt nothing, but I wondered if we did catch Levaseur's team if I wouldn't jump from my sled to his and tear at it with my teeth.

We rocketed down the last hill, and then we emerged onto the lake. And the dogs now saw the other team clearly. Nothing to it. Nothing to do. I pumped and we ran and my dogs, Fred's dogs, my team, ran faster than Levaseur's. I knew it. We rounded the far turn and headed back, and I shouted for them to take us home, go home, and that was all it took. We began to gain in feet and yards and then the blue jacket danced in front of me.

"Trail!" I yelled.

And he was a gentleman. He braked his team and I yelled, "On by, Charlie!" Then I did start to cry because Charlie glided by, and Willow, and the big boys in back, and Jerry smiled at me. Twenty years running, what he knew, what he felt, I could only guess. I wanted to say that I loved him, I loved his dogs, but we went by and I shouted for us to go home again. "Home, girls! Home, boys!" Snow filled the space between us. And we became the dancing jacket, the ghost team.

I wanted to run forever. I wanted to die on the sled and stay there forever.

Then we came up the last hill, back into the woods, back in sight of the finish. People shouted, not many, but some, and I knew no one would catch us now. Then something fluttered. Nothing big, nothing I really noticed, but Charlie stopped. The other dogs stopped, too, and Willow tried to tug left. It made no sense. The finish line stood no more than twenty feet from us, and I shouted, "On by!"

They wouldn't move. I stood for a second, five seconds, watching them pant, their red tongues out, snow swirling like a dream, and I couldn't believe what I saw. Then I heard Fred's voice, Fred's voice over everyone, yelling for me to run them in. I didn't know what he meant, but I heard dogs coming up the hill behind me, clearing the woods, and I jumped off the sled. I ran to the front of the team, grabbed the neckline between Willow and Charlie, and began to pull. They came forward gladly enough, relieved to have a direction, and I ran as hard as I could. Then it became a movie, because I knew Levaseur's team had us beat, knew we could not match their momentum, and as hard as I ran I felt them pass. I kept running. And in a second we finished, passing over the line nearly on Levaseur's runners. People clapped for my effort, but I turned back to the dogs.

"Good boys, good girls," I said, because I did not want them to take the defeat into their hearts.

Dogs do not like things above them.

Someone had raised the finish flag and that's what stopped them.

Fred explained it. He said it happens often. Someone had sent a little kid out to do the flag, and he had raised it up, more or less in the sight line of my dogs, and they had balked. A flutter like that could send dogs completely off the trail. On the finish line, you are supposed to lift the flag up and backward, not down and forward like an ax.

Greg, the president, gave me a blue second-place ribbon.

People clapped. My heart felt hollow. The irony was that I had almost won anyway, despite my dogs stopping. I had almost caught Jerry's team on time, but he had won by a few seconds. If I had jumped off and run immediately, I probably would have edged him out.

I slipped outside and had a cigarette. An older woman, maybe fifty, smoked behind the building, around the corner and out of the wind. I stood next to her. She wore an enormous hat thing. It made her look like she was a bottle and someone had squeezed a top on her.

"What a way to spend a weekend, huh?" she said. "This cold."

"The dogs like it," I said.

She nodded.

"You ever notice," she said, puffing, "that we make up things to tell ourselves. Like, we tell ourselves that fishing is better in the rain because we need to believe that to go out in the rain. Or if a bird craps on you, it's good luck. How do we know a dog wouldn't rather be sitting on a couch eating a big bowl of popcorn and watching TV?"

I smiled. Then I couldn't keep from laughing. The woman looked ridiculous, but I liked her.

"Sounds good to me," I said.

"Cold," she said.

Bobby says he never trusts anyone who hasn't smoked at some point in his or her life. He said people who never smoke lack imagination. He says cigarettes are life's punctuation. Bobby sometimes gets carried away with his words.

I sat in the back with Sebastian's head on my lap. The wind lifted snow off the sides of the road. It created an illusion. Maybe we traveled forward, or maybe we made no progress at all. I leaned my forehead against the window and let the cold pass from outside to my forehead and then down to my face and neck.

Up front, Mary and Fred talked. They talked about drivers and teams and gossip. Nothing big. But I liked hearing their voices. And I liked Sebastian's large head on my lap, his huffy breathing as he slept. The dials on the dashboard glimmered green.

We all worked together to put the dogs to bed when we got back. A thermometer on a post near the equipment shed said it had gone to ten below zero. The dogs got out and went into their sleep barrels. I could barely move my hands or fingers, and my legs ached from pumping the sled. Snow squeaked under our boots on the way back to the house.

The house had lost its heat and light. For a second, when we came in, we couldn't tell. But a moment later we realized the heat had cut out. Fred said maybe a power line had gone down in the storm. It killed to have the house cold and Fred cursed once, sharp and quick, and then went down to the basement. He wore a headlamp he used for working with the dogs.

"The pipes will burst if there's no heat," Mary said, grabbing candles. "Come on, we'll build a fire in the woodstove."

We heard Fred moving around down in the basement. She handed me a candle and we walked together like pioneer women, our hands cupped around the flickering flames.

We laid a fire in the stove. Mary used old paint sticks as tinder. We got it going on the first match. Mary added small pieces of pine until the flame couldn't resist growing. It didn't push any heat at first, but the flames provided light. Sebastian clicked around the bare floors, his claws tapping on the wood. His eyes glowed when the candlelight hit them.

Fred came up a few minutes later.

"The pipes look okay," he said. "The electricity must have just cut out a short time ago."

"Well, then," Mary said, "there's nothing to worry about. We'll just have to stay close to the woodstove."

"When life gives you lemons," Fred said, "call the attorneys."

"Who's hungry?" Mary asked. "Suddenly I'm famished."

She carried a candle into the kitchen. Fred and I heard her rummaging around. Then she came out carrying a tray loaded with bread and chips, a plastic container of black olives, three root beers, mustard, mayonnaise, and a block of cheese. She put it on the coffee table. Then she searched around behind the woodstove and found some metal gadgets.

"Ever use one of these?" she asked me. "Sandwich makers? You can hold them over the fire. We used to use them when Nicky was younger, but we haven't used them in years."

"I'd forgotten we had them," Fred said.

"They should be washed, but we're camping," Mary said. "I guess the heat will kill anything too lively. Wipe them down with a paper towel."

"And you just hold them over the heat?" I asked.

"That's it," Mary said. "Now go ahead and build your sandwich. You can design your own."

We piled on stuff between two bread slices, then clamped them in the sandwich gadgets. The woodstove already pushed a wave of heat toward us. I put the edge of the sandwich maker on the stove and pretty soon the cheese began to melt. It smelled delicious. Fred's sandwich kept falling apart, and each time it did he had to pluck the gunk off the surface with a pair of stove mitts. It was funny to watch him being a little clumsy.

When we all had our sandwiches cooked, we sat back in the big couch they have and watched the stove and ate. You could feel anyplace away from the stove would be cold, but right there, right in the fan of heat that pushed away from the logs, everything was good and warm. And it was good to see Fred and Mary eating in a kind of sloppy, kid way. We ate everything on the tray Mary had brought out. But even after we finished, no one left and turned in for bed.

10

Bobby stepped out from behind the kennel.

It was midmorning. I had Laika with me. I had mucked out the cages. The temperature had wandered up to twenty-eight and it felt almost like summer. I worked with just a vest on and leather work gloves. When Bobby first stepped out, I couldn't quite place him. That sounds nutty, I know, but he was entirely out of context.

Bobby, here.

My mind couldn't get around it. Bobby in New Hampshire. Bobby in snow. He wore a jean jacket and his old black pants and his cruddy boots. No hat, no gloves. He looked thinner, like someone had pressed his parts closer, tighter. He smiled.

"Let's go," he said.

"Where?" I asked.

What I meant was, how?

"I've got a car out on the road," he said. "I've been sitting around freezing my ass off waiting for you. Then I had to get you alone."

"How long have you been here?"

"I've been here all weekend. Come on. Let's get out of here."

He grabbed my hand. And I went with him.

He didn't kiss me. Or say anything soft. He just took my hand and I followed.

And Laika followed me.

Fate mixed it all up. If Bobby hadn't emerged right then; if Laika hadn't been out of her cage; if I had had a moment to think, a second, I would have made different choices. I might still have gone with Bobby, but I wouldn't have taken Laika. Laika had no business being with Bobby.

I dropped the poop shovel and went with him. We followed his tracks in the snow. Laika chugged along behind. She was enough of a puppy to need us to break trail. She jumped from one footstep to the next. I remember thinking that Bobby looked out of place in the snow. Way out of place. But he was shrewd enough to keep back toward the woods, out of sight from the house. I could have told him we didn't need to worry. Fred and Mary had run to town. We could have strolled out the front door, but Bobby didn't know that. And besides, I guess, they could have come back at any moment. It made sense to keep to the trees.

His car looked like a piece of crap. I didn't recognize it, though. It wasn't Paulie's or Killy's or any of the people's cars I usually knew. I didn't ask him, either. I felt like suddenly I was back in the old way, just hustling, and a laugh started down in my throat that became a little hysterical. It was Bobby who made me understand that Laika was right there with us. I knew she was, of course, but I hadn't fully taken it in. If we left, she would be out on the road. That's what I realized.

I opened the door and she hopped in. Then Bobby cranked the engine. He wheeled around and made a big deal of skidding on purpose. I grabbed a pack of cigarettes off the dash and lit one. The whole time I had a knot in my stomach. I started to cry as I smoked and when Bobby saw me, he patted my knee.

"I came as fast as I could," he said.

And I couldn't tell him that's not why I was crying.

I couldn't tell him exactly why I was crying, because I didn't know myself.

A funny thing about Bobby I had never noticed before: he drives like an old man. His hands rest at two and ten, and he never goes over the speed limit. He also presses the gas, lets up, presses it again. He's not a good driver. And he hunches at the wheel like a snake folded in an S.

"We can't go to Worcester," I said. "They'll pick us up in about ten seconds."

"I got to get this back to Burlington," he said. "The car."

"Whose is it?"

"A girl's."

"What girl?"

He smirked at me.

"Tell me what girl, Bobby," I said.

"Luanne. You don't know her."

"How do you know her?"

"I met her around. She's a friend of Paulie's sister."

"Did you sleep with her?"

He frowned and made a disgusted face.

"No," he said.

"Are you lying?"

"No," he said, and lit a cigarette.

I looked at him. Laika found something in the backseat and started chewing it. Bobby glanced in the rearview mirror, then swung his hand back and hit her. His hand thudded against her side and she moved across the seat.

"Don't ever hit her," I said, turning to her.

"She's chewing."

"Don't hit her."

He looked at me.

"I didn't sleep with her," he said.

Bobby's father hit him. He also gave him Dutchman's rubs. A Dutchman's rub is when you grab someone in a headlock, knuckle your finger, and rub it back and forth on the person's skull. Sometimes Bobby's father would say "Knock, knock" as he gave him the rub. His father worked in a mill making paint stirrers out of birch logs. He worked a lathe. Bobby made really beautiful models out of paint stirrers, Popsicle sticks, anything birch. Planes, birds, kites, towns, trucks. One day Bobby's dad gave him a Dutchman's rub so bad he split Bobby's scalp. The doctors tried to figure how hard you would have to rub to even do that, to split a scalp. They said they couldn't imagine it.

I think Bobby's dad rubbed himself into Bobby's head. I think Bobby's dad slithered right inside Bobby's brain. That's why he needed to open his son's scalp. So he could get inside.

•

I pulled Laika up and let her sleep on my lap. We drove across country roads, following a river. The countryside sagged under the snow and warmer temperatures. Bobby listened to a Sum 41 CD. I put my head against the window and felt sleepy and crazy at once. I pictured what Fred and Mary would say when they found me gone. I pictured them walking through the house, checking things, knowing inside what had happened but not wanting to come out and say it. They had experience in this sort of thing, I understood, but it still probably felt shitty. What I couldn't think about was Fred going down and finding Laika gone. It had been stupid to take her, and he would know that. That was something he might not forgive. And I thought of Laika running on a team, the snow flying, the intent gaze of the dogs as they went ahead. She would miss that. She wouldn't know it. I had taken that away.

Then for a while I stared out at the countryside and pictured a sled running on the hills beside the river. I imagined driving it, braking, angling, pumping. I pictured the dogs running and every sound in the world pushed away. Just dogs. And wind, and pines sometimes rubbing together.

Big Mac wrapper, fries box, milk-shake cup, salt packets, straw wrapper, two empty packs of Marlboros, a folded map, Hershey bar wrapper, an empty can of Dr. Pepper, an empty plastic bottle of Red Bull. All like a tide pool at the bottom of the car, all a wading pool where we put our feet.

"Luanne has a gargoyle suit," Bobby said. "She has two, actually.

And she puts them on, and there's this street in Burlington. Street-art stuff. And she puts them on and she stands on a bucket, real quiet, and she waits until people notice her."

"She puts both suits on?" I asked, half sleepy.

"No, of course not," Bobby said, reaching to the dashboard for a cigarette. "She puts on one and waits."

"And it takes a long time for people to notice her?"

He looked at me. If looks could kill.

He said, "Jesus, you're being hardheaded."

"I just don't see what you're talking about."

He took some of his cigarette. He didn't reach over and touch Laika. Except to hit her, he hadn't touched her at all.

"She puts on one suit, and if someone else wants to help, you can put the other one on, and she pretends to be stone. That's what she does. And people throw money in a tip jar to have their picture taken with her. Kids are all scared and everything, so it's kind of funny. She moves like a scary stone creature, you know. Like a vampire sort of."

"How much does she make?" I asked.

"Well, this time of year it's pretty cold out. But a lot."

"How much?"

He took a long drag on his cigarette and blew it toward the windshield. I could tell I pissed him off with all the questions. Bobby doesn't like to think too hard about the practical side of things. His face looked knotted and bored. He reached out and turned up the radio. I turned it down.

"Sorry," I said, "I just wondered."

"Gargoyles are big right now. And angels. One girl is an angel and she makes a pile. She does all this stuff, you know, with a wand and a halo. People think it's really funny."

"I've never been to Burlington," I said.

"It's cool," he said. "Lots of street people."

I put my nose on the top of Laika's head. She smelled like straw and snow.

Burlington sat on Lake Champlain. Coming down off the highway, you could see the city and the white bulge of the lake behind it. Laika sat up. Maybe she could tell the car moved slower or had changed speeds. I told Bobby to pull into a Burger King. We went through the drive-in and bought a cheeseburger meal. They give you two for one, plus fries. Bobby ate one, and I split the other with Laika. She ate it in two quick bites. Then she looked around for more. I gave her fries. I made her eat them slowly. Her hindquarters shivered when she ate.

I tied string to Laika as a leash, but then made Bobby give me his belt. A string wouldn't hold her. We parked on a side street. The houses on either side looked short and ugly. You could tell no one had any money. Most of the houses had an old car to the side or a motorcycle sitting under a tarp. Laika peed on the lawn as soon as we stepped out.

"Which house is it?" I asked.

Bobby pointed to a gray one.

"She rents the basement," he said. "It's okay."

"Does she live alone?"

He shook his head.

"A couple older guys live upstairs. Biker guys. It's okay, though. Larry and Phil. You'll get to know them."

"Are they going to be okay with Laika?" I asked.

"You shouldn't have brought the dog," Bobby said.

Bobby left me standing on the street while he went to find Luanne. Compared to the weekend, it wasn't cold. Laika sniffed around the curb. I walked her slowly, letting her get her bearings. Pretty soon Bobby came back. Laika skittered back from him because he moved too fast.

"You can come in," he said. "I don't know."

"What do you mean, you don't know?"

"It's just, you know."

"How many people are in there?"

"Just her right now. Danny lives there and so does Pierre, this wicked French guy."

"Real French?"

"French Canadian."

"Jesus, Bobby."

"It's a place to sleep," he said.

"What about Laika?"

"You can't bring the dog inside. But there's an old pole on the side of the house. You can tie him up there."

"Her."

"Her, then."

"Is there any kind of shelter for her?"

He flashed, "Listen, I'm not a pet store, you know. I don't know this place that well."

"Calm down, Bobby."

"I came and got you," he said. "Doesn't that count for something?"

"Sure," I said.

The only memory I have of my father is the day he showed me a round scar he had on his rib cage. He said he had been riding his bike down a hill and the bike hit a rock and went down. He rammed into the handlebar. The handlebar didn't have any grips, so the round end of the metal went right into his rib cage. Not far but enough to scar him.

He showed me the scar on a summer day. He had filled up a kiddie pool and knelt next to it while I played. Tree leaves swirled around his head whenever I looked up at him. That's my memory, anyway. He looked dark and thin. His arms had blue tattoos on them. He made his hands go under the water, then squirt up the water like a whale. "Look, Baby," he would say and when I leaned in, the water pumped up like magic.

Someone had tied a dog to the pole a hundred years ago. The pole looked rusty. We didn't have a chain or a proper tie out. I had to use Bobby's belt and a four-feet-long piece of clothesline. Laika didn't like it one bit. She shuddered around the pole and began whimpering as soon as we began to walk away.

"Sorry, sweetie," I said to her, looking at the pole and the deep snow around it.

"She'll be okay," Bobby said.

"I'm not so sure."

"We'll get her fixed up tomorrow."

"Are we staying here?" I asked.

He shrugged.

I felt something get heavy and sick in my belly.

"Not for long," he said, looking at me.

If you can do it, you can put one foot out as far as possible, point your toe, then spin. Like a ballerina. And if you do it fast enough, your foot will trace a perfect circle around the center of your body. It's easiest on the beach, in sand, but you can do it in snow.

Laika's leash made a perfect circle in the snow.

Laika's circle consisted of thirty-seven steps.

11

Luanne's breasts were bigger than mine. She had reddish red hair and white skin. When I walked in and saw her sitting on the kitchen counter, talking to someone on a cell phone, she lifted her chin to say hello to me. She held a cigarette in the hand that didn't hold the cell phone. The kitchen floor was dirty. Paper bags full of empty beer cans leaned against the kitchen counters. Even though it was cold out, a few flies buzzed and hit against the cans, making a sound like smoke going through a chimney.

Bobby grabbed us two beers out of the fridge. He handed me one.

When Luanne hung up, she said, "You're Baby?"

I nodded.

"The way Bobby talked about you, I thought you'd be different."

"Different how?"

She shrugged.

Different, more pretty, I thought. Different, taller. Different.

"Sorry," I said.

"Nothing to be sorry about. I've been in foster care. Juvey, you name it. When Bobby said he needed to borrow a car, I let him. Because I've been in, you know?"

"I know. Thanks."

"They think they're doing you such a freaking favor, when all you really want is to be left alone."

I nodded.

She turned on the sink faucet and doused her cigarette. Then she slid the dead butt into an empty beer can.

"You can use the gargoyle suit to make a little money," she said. "Days I'm not using it, I mean. You can get ahead a little."

"Okay," I said. "Bobby told you I have a dog."

"No dogs," she said.

"I understand."

The beer tasted good.

Pierre said to me, "The real money is in the back-window scam. What we do is we get you girls, you and Luanne, we get you set up like hookers. I've got a friend over at this motel. It's a shit box, but he can give you a room cheap on certain days. Then you get some guy to walk you back. You ask him for money up front. When you tell him you want to go into the bathroom to get ready, he'll let you. Then you open the window and climb out the back. Just like that. The guy is sitting there watching some ass TV show, thinking you're about to come prancing back in, when you're already down the block. Me and Bobby can be outside to help you through the window. No fuss, no muss. What's the guy going to do? He can't go to the motel management, right? What's he going to say? Even if he did go to someone at the motel, it would be my friend, and my friend would get all 'What do you mean you had a prostitute in there?' and that would be that. I'm telling you. Pro girls around here get one hundred bucks for like an hour. You could get a hundred and not even have to touch the old bastards, just slip out the window."

Pierre was a pothead dude. He smoked a joint as he talked. He had dreadlocks and wore pants that came way down to his butt crack. He smelled. He needed to bathe. And he talked too much.

Bobby didn't hear Pierre talk about climbing through back windows and pretending to be a prostitute. Bobby played a video game. He sat on a chair with the toggle flipping right and left. Sometimes when he came to an important part of the game, he stretched his body out as if he braced for a car crash that had to come one way or another.

Danny weighed at least two hundred and seventy pounds. And he hardly talked. He looked like every beer he had ever drunk still hung on him. He ate chips, and when he had most of them gone, he tore open the bag and used his pointer finger to touch the salt, bring it to his mouth, touch the salt, bring it to his mouth, touch the salt. It looked like he wanted to give the food a direction to go in, mostly toward his belly.

Danny had dropped out of the University of Vermont. He had studied philosophy, then early childhood education, then nothing at all. He lived for almost a year in the dorms without going to school. He sold pot and he bought beer for kids. His parents didn't care. They said he needed to make his choices. That's what Luanne told me later, when all the boys sat staring at the video game. Something in

Danny had died, I thought. Down in his belly. And all the food in the world wouldn't bring it back alive.

I heard her on the edge of things. Way out. Then it got louder and I knew it was Laika. She whined and cried and barked. You could tell, just by listening, that she hated being outside alone. I got up and put on my shoes and threw on a jacket.

Bobby said, "She'll be okay. She has to learn."

Beer still hung on his words.

"Be right back," I said.

I went out the back door, down the steps, and saw her. She sprang up against the tie out. Her paws waved in front of her. All the misery in the world, I thought, right in her loneliness. "You're okay," I said.

But she wasn't. Ice covered her coat, and the snow ranged too deep. She could not get around the pole. The line jammed into the bottom portion, packed the snow on itself, and made it shorter and shorter for her.

I pulled the line free of the snow so she would have more room. Then I ran my hands over her body so the ice would come off. I couldn't tell what time it was. I wanted it to be light, for the sun to come up, so she would not feel so lonely. I told her I would be back in the morning.

"You're okay," I said, then headed off back to the house.

But I only got a few feet away before she really started to cry and pull at the tie out.

"What do you want?" I said.

I felt the beer in my head. I felt the cigarettes in my chest.

I wanted to kick her quiet.

I took her to Luanne's car and put her in the backseat. I shut the door. For a minute she jumped up against the windows. But I backed away. The temperature felt below zero. A steady wind came down the street and threw things ahead of it. I turned my back into it and watched Laika jump against the car window, nearly silent, nearly gone from me.

Bobby says money is only paper and you should not respect it any more than you respect other paper. He says a million dollars would not change you, the inside you, one iota. Money can change behavior, he says, but not the core person. He said this when I heard on the radio about a young guy who started a cord wood charity. This young guy learned about an old couple that had frozen to death in Vermont because they couldn't afford to pay their heating bill. So this guy decided he would get people to donate wood and stoves. That way, the guy figured, old people would at least have that heat.

Bobby says wood is money, only thicker. It's all paper.

Snoring. A TV fizzing on static. The bump and hum of a refrigerator. Something small and delicate eating from a chip bag. A clock ticking. Heat coming on, a chug down in the basement, then something rattling in the pipes, heat rising. Wind going over the house, looking for things left behind. A sigh. Another sigh. Someone speaking in a dream murmur.

12

Once upon a time, a man named Lord Tweedmouth lived in the border area of Scotland. He hunted grouse on the weekend and kept spaniels to accompany him. He was proud of his dogs, and of his staff, and therein the story begins.

A Russian circus came to entertain the local population. One of the acrobats fell in love with a servant on Lord Tweedmouth's staff. Lord Tweedmouth heard of the romance and called the woman servant to him.

"You may not see this Russian acrobat," he said. "He is a man who will do you no good. Leave him, or leave my service."

The woman servant refused to see the acrobat afterward.

In spite, the Russian acrobat slipped a Russian wolfhound into Lord Tweedmouth's kennel. The wolfhound—who is five times taller than the tallest spaniel—impregnated the smaller dogs. After a few months passed, and long after the circus had departed, the spaniels gave birth to beautiful blonde dogs. The dogs possessed a spaniel's kind temperament, the carriage of a wolfhound, and the wavy coat of a water retriever.

That was how the golden retriever came to be.

That's what I read in a book at the Potters' house.

put gargoyles all over the building. Even though it was a Christian building, a church, I mean, they still put pagan symbols on it."

I nodded.

"I love gargoyles," Luanne said.

After we posed for about ten minutes, a woman came by with two kids. She was probably hurrying them home after school, but when they saw us, they sprinted over. The woman didn't have a camera or anything. She smiled at us. It was a tight smile, as if to say she had enough to deal with, now here we were, haunting her children.

"Come on, boys," she said.

Luanne put her long fingers over the closest one's shoulders. He screamed.

I wonder what it means to love gargoyles. I wonder what it means to want to turn to stone.

We ate a bowl of split-pea soup in Sweet Tomatoes, sitting at the bar. It was funny. We had our heads sitting on stools on either side of us. Our long tails curled up behind us. Our costumes are stone-colored, greenish-moss-colored. Luanne made me wear two napkins—one around my neck, the other on my lap—to keep my costume clean.

Laika stayed outside where I could see her. People passed and petted her. We kept the buckets next to her.

"You and Bobby have been together how long?" she asked.

"A year or so."

"Wow," she said. "The longest I've ever been with a guy is about three months."

She spooned her soup up.

"It's because we've been through a lot, I guess," I said. "We met at a group therapy session. That kind of thing."

"You should keep Bobby away from Pierre," she said after a few seconds. "Pierre is into heavy stuff."

"Like what?"

"Drugs. Coke. And he deals, so if he gets caught, it's going to burn. He wants Bobby to deal for him."

"How do you know that?"

She shrugged. She said, "It's good money, dealing."

"You think Bobby would do it?"

"He's got to do something," she said. "And that's the easiest thing there is. Besides, Bobby thinks he's all that, tough guy, you know. But he's not."

"I know," I said.

"Pierre wants me to do that thing with the guys," she said.

"Climbing through the motel window?"

She nodded."It's a hundred bucks for doing nothing," she said.

"I don't trust that setup. It's a pretty screwed-up thing to do anyway, you know."

She ate more soup. A gargoyle eating soup on a cold day in Vermont.

Before we went back up on the buckets, I called Fred and Mary.

I timed it so they would be out with the dogs. And that seemed to work. I heard the phone ring a few times, then heard the answering machine pick up. I got a little tongue-tied, but then I told them fast that Laika was okay, I didn't mean to take her, I was sorry about that, I meant no offense by it, or by leaving for that matter, and sorry. Then I hung up.

$43.63. For being stone. Split two ways. Minus the soup.

Larry and Phil came downstairs. They brought a thirty-pack and two big joints. Larry is probably thirty-five or so, and Phil is even older. Larry is the loud one, and Phil is the sidekick.

Bobby says everyone has a sidekick.

One guy has to be the Lone Ranger, the other guy Tonto. One is Batman, the other Robin.

No doubt Bobby thinks I'm his sidekick.

Way back in Phil's eyes, you can tell he thinks they're stupid for hanging with a bunch of teenagers. Larry doesn't care, even if he knows it's cheap behavior. Larry has a ponytail and is Harleyed out. Leather vest. Harley tattoo on the arm. His tattoo must have gotten Bobby thinking, because he made me pull down my pants enough to show off my tiger. Larry whistled. Luanne put her finger on my butt and traced the tiger stripes to see if it really spelled Bobby.

It did.

Both the guys kind of propped up Pierre while they knocked down Danny. I had to watch a while to see how it happened. They started mocking Pierre, but it was just a stepping-stone to Danny. They kidded Pierre, but that kidding had a funny, light air to it. The kidding they did with Danny was mean. I could tell it hurt him. Sometimes Pierre joined in. Somehow, by being kidded first, he thought he had a right to join in on Danny.

Danny's face turns red when he becomes the center of anything. He drinks beer like a baby calf sucking at a bottle. His throat moves. And he pulls the liquid in with his lips.

Danny has no flight response at all.

If Bobby is a dump dog, and my mother is a wolf, then Danny is the dumb dog that stays and gets clobbered for wanting too much out of the dump.

Larry and Phil liked looking at Luanne and me. You could tell. Larry more than Phil, but you knew they watched you. Young chicks. Young, stupid chicks, that's what they thought. They told a few stories about being on Harleys. We were supposed to think they were cool, but they weren't. They were losers.

Pierre told them the about the motel-window scam.

"You better check that window a couple times before you do that," Larry said. "Windows get stuck this time of year."

"We'll check it," Pierre said.

Then Larry looked right at me. He said, "You lay down with dogs, you get up with fleas."

Later he pulled out a joint. We all smoked. Larry took short, quick hits. The guys tried to do it just like him. After a little while, I went into the one bedroom and used the phone. I called Cindy's home number. She picked up on the third ring.

"Hello?" she asked.

"It's Baby," I said.

"Baby, where are you?"

"Somewhere."

"Are you safe?"

"Yes," I said.

"Why are you calling? I mean if you're safe and happy."

That was supposed to shock me to my senses. The grand truth and all that. Tough woman.

I said, "I wanted to know if you found my mother."

"Not yet."

"Tell the truth—are you actually looking for her?"

"People are looking. I won't kid you and say it's a full-time job for anyone. Occasionally, people check records and data banks. Like I said, she can stay gone if she wants to."

"Would you know it if she died?"

"Maybe. Probably not. If she went out to Oregon, say, or Idaho, I doubt it. If she stayed in New England, we might have a chance. It's a long shot, Baby."

"That's what gets me. Thinking she might be dead and no one knows."

She didn't answer.

Then she said, "The Potters were surprised you left. They thought you liked the dogs and everything."

"I did."

"Did Bobby show up?"

I didn't say anything.

"Here's the thing," Cindy said. "Think about what's going to happen, Baby. I know Bobby. I've read his record. He hasn't had an easy run either."

"So?"

"So where does it all lead? Where are you going? Let me guess. Right now you have a few bucks and maybe you flopped at someone's house. But that won't last forever. So you're going to have to come up with some way to make money. You're fifteen. You don't have a high school diploma. You tell me. Where do you think it will go?"

"Not everyone wants to get somewhere," I said. "You think we're going somewhere, but really we're just going around in circles."

"That's a nice, convenient cynical view."

"It's the only view."

"Meanwhile, you have to eat and you have to have shelter. It's the way of the world."

"Your world," I said.

We didn't speak for a few seconds. I heard the line go static and then back. She talked on a cell, I guessed.

"The Potters told me to tell you they would like the dog back," she said. "That's the only thing they were disappointed about."

"Tell them she's okay. I didn't mean to take the dog."

"Still," she said.

"I'll try."

"The dog has a home. It didn't volunteer to be homeless, you know."

"Screw you," I said.

"Okay, maybe that was a little mean. I didn't like your remarks about Catie. Maybe I'm still annoyed with you."

Bobby came in, looked at me on the phone, and sat beside me.

"I have to go," I said.

"You want to give me a number? Anything?"

"I have to go," I repeated.

She didn't hang up, though. I did.

"We should go to Mexico," I told Bobby.

We still sat next to the phone. A little light came in through the door crack. People talked out in the kitchen. Larry talked the most, but Pierre talked a lot, too.

"When?" he asked.

"Right now. Soon. Let's get someplace where it's warm."

"Okay," he said.

"When?"

"Soon," he said.

"When, though? We can't stay here forever. Luanne said we needed to make plans."

"I'm working on some things," he said. "We need some money to travel."

"Don't start dealing," I said. "That's a bad plan, Bobby."

He didn't say anything.

"And I'm not doing that window thing," I said, "so don't even think about it."

"Luanne is going to."

"Then she's an idiot."

He said, "A hundred bucks for nothing."

"Nothing's for nothing, Bobby."

Then he said something mean. "Whoa," he said. "Baby gets deep."

"Get over yourself, Bobby."

Then he started getting affectionate. But I didn't feel that way. I got up and went back into the kitchen. And when I saw the people there, I kept going and went outside to see Laika.

Thirty-seven steps around her pole. That's the circle she ran. The cord and leash had pushed down the snow so now she stood in a moon crater, the rim just beyond her reached higher than her chest.

I sang her a silly song.

She sat and put her paws on my legs. Licked my face. When I stood, she wanted to come with me. It was seven degrees and the wind had picked up.

"I'm sorry you can't come inside," I said. "You probably miss all the boys and girls back at Fred and Mary's, don't you?"

She barked. She barked even more when I went back to the house.

14

We didn't work during the week, but on Saturday Luanne and I spent all morning on the buckets being gargoyles. The sun had come out and it was a good day, the temperature up around thirty-five. People wanted to be outside. A few streeties showed up to play music and two guys, Frank and Frank, they called themselves, did juggling and balancing acts about fifty feet away. They walked on stilts so it was easy to see them.

A Christian guy came by and tried to convert us. He said the statues were ungodly. He said we were encouraging demon worship. He was a fatty-watty, with a big roll of blubber right under his belt. His chin wattled when he talked to us. Luanne hissed at him. She made me laugh.

Bobby came by with Pierre at noon. They both looked high. Bobby had copped some fake ID so he could get into the bars around town. He liked going to this place where Phish got their start, this bar just off Church Street, and that's where Pierre did his business. He sold joints, sometimes a little coke. He had Ecstasy, too, but not on a regular basis. Larry and Phil supplied it, though no one ever came out and said so.

I was hoping Bobby would take me to lunch, spend a little time with me, but he and Pierre blasted right by after hanging with us for a few seconds. They had to go somewhere. They took Luanne with them to show her the motel setup. It was supposed to happen tonight. I wanted no part of it.

The Black Crow Bookstore let people bring dogs inside, so I went down there for lunch with Laika. They had a large upstairs store, all new books, but down below, down in the basement, they sold secondhand stuff. The manager downstairs—a guy named Wally—had greasy hair and white skin, and he wore glasses about as thick as the heels on a pair of men's shoes. When he read, he held the book up close to his face, like he was going to kiss it, but that was because of his eyes. I liked him, though, and twice he brought biscuits for Laika. He had a dog at home named Lonny. A border collie.

He wasn't there on Saturday, at least I didn't see him, so I sat on one of the old leather chairs and ate my sandwich. I gave pieces to Laika, and when I finished, I pulled down a book on barns. I never much cared what I looked at when I had lunch at the Black Crow because each book had something, you could always get interested, if you just gave it a few seconds. I didn't want novels or stories. I liked paging through big coffee-table books, ones with pictures so true you could sort of fall into them. I didn't care about barns, really, but when someone took good pictures of them, you had to pay attention.

I got drowsy in the heat and fell asleep, I guess, because the next thing I knew, Wally was right in front of me, down on his haunches, giving a biscuit to Laika. I sat up fast, alarmed, but then I remembered where I was. Wally smiled. He petted Laika's head.

"I have a book for you," he said.

"Really?" I asked.

"I knew I knew the name from somewhere. Your dog's name, I mean. Do you know what Laika stands for?"

I shook my head.

"Laika means 'Little Curly.' Laika was the first space dog. The first dog in space for the Russians. Actually, she was the first living organism to leave the earth's atmosphere. That's what your dog was named after."

"Are you kidding me?"

"No. Didn't you know? I figured you knew if you named her that."

I looked down at her. She watched Wally for more biscuits.

Wally's walkie-talkie squawked and he had to hustle off. Before he left, he told me the book was mine to keep. A present. He put the book on top of the book in my lap.

Luanne came and got me before I could read any of the book about Laika.

"Time to be stone," she said.

She said that because Pierre and Bobby had smoked her up. It was a joke on being stoned.

She usually liked looking at a book on the construction of Notre Dame. Gargoyles. She never got tired of it. But she didn't look at it that afternoon. She glanced at my book about Laika. She laughed when I told her Wally had given the book to me.

"Wally's got a crush on you," she said.

"You're daft," I said, which is what British people say.

•

They put Laika in her space capsule four days before they launched her. She could not move or stand. She ate jellied food and eliminated into a bag.

A guy pinched my ass late that afternoon. We had almost stopped when he came up behind me and pinched it.

I swung around and tried to punch him.

"Sorry," he said, dodging, "I thought you were a statue."

"Screw off," I said.

But the distraction caused me to lose my balance. I fell and came down whack on my elbow. Luanne cursed him out good after that, but my elbow hurt like hell anyway.

It was weird.

I helped Luanne get dressed for the motel scam. It kind of felt like we were getting her ready to go out on a big date or something, but instead, she was going to pretend to be a hooker. She tried on three things, and that was crazy when you thought about what she was doing it for. At one point, we both laughed because she tried to be this babe-hooker.

I didn't try to talk her out of it. People are going to do whatever they decide to do and you can't talk them out of it. I didn't waste my breath.

Danny did, though. I liked him for it. When she stepped out of the bedroom looking hot as hell, Danny looked up from the TV and didn't take his eyes off her. I realized that maybe he had a thing for her. He shook his head, and you could tell he wanted to say something.

"You look beautiful," he said, for starters.

"Thank you, Danny," she said, and did a little curtsy. Her skirt was way short.

"I don't think you should do it," Danny said. "Too many variables. Too much can go wrong."

"Pierre and Bobby will be right there," she said.

"They're already baked. Please don't do it," he said.

Strange, but it was a little too personal. Obviously it came from his feeling toward her. He didn't want to see her tarted up and attracting men.

"I'll be okay," Luanne said.

"Ask Baby what she thinks."

Luanne looked at me.

"Your decision," I said.

You can make a decision without consciously ever making a decision. When she put on her coat and stepped outside, it was over.

The temperature had dipped some, but it still wasn't bad. I made Luanne wait while I went and played with Laika a second. Laika hated the pole and tried to pull free when I went near her, but I calmed her down the way Fred showed me. You take your hand and stretch it flat and you press it at the bottom of a dog's belly. Wolves do that. When one wolf returns from a hunt, he or she goes around and nudges the other dogs in the belly. It's a signal that everything is okay. So that's what I did to Laika. She sat eventually and looked at me.

"Come on," Luanne yelled from the front of the house.

I went. I closed my ears to the sound of Laika jumping against the chain.

A strange thing happened on the way to meet up with Pierre and Bobby.

I saw Nicky.

It happened so fast I hardly believed it. We had just come around the corner of the Abercrombie & Fitch store when he passed me. Perpendicular. If we had been in the movies, the film would have stopped to slow motion and we would have had a significant look as snow fell. But snow didn't fall, and our glance was quick and random. I took two steps forward before I realized it really was Nicky. He looked handsome as hell, as usual, and he had an amazing-looking woman on his arm. They walked with their heads together, cutting into the wind, and I thought of him with his jazz CD and his forest green Tacoma. And it bothered me that he saw me with Luanne—her all tarty—and he probably thought we looked like a pair of losers.

He recognized me, though. I saw that.

His eyes went over me, then they came back and fixed on me. It probably took him a second to click in the name and face out of context. I felt my stomach ball up, ready for a confrontation, but he kept going. A second later he was the back of a coat heading away.

"Crap," I said.

"What's wrong?" Luanne asked.

I told her.

"You sure he recognized you?" she asked.

"Positive," I said.

We both knew what that meant. It was time to get moving. Burlington wasn't safe anymore for Bobby and me.

Laika was a street dog in Moscow before the Russian scientists captured her along with a troop of mutts. They trained her for sustained flight by putting her into smaller and smaller cages. Different dogs adapted in varying degrees. Laika was not the top candidate, but she was pretty good. The Russians shot other dogs almost out of the atmosphere. They went up and down, then splashed into the ocean. America did the same thing with its space program. But in *Sputnik II,* the Russians decided to send a living organism beyond our atmosphere. Until something ventured into space, the idea of space travel remained theoretical. Laika changed that.

15

My mother fell in love with a fellow named Marty. She thought he was going to be dependable and good. Solid. She talked herself into being in love with Marty, figuring a guy like Marty would lend stability to our lives. Marty wore jeans, mostly, and button-down shirts. He worked at a computer store, doing retail sales. Mom met him when she went in to buy a mouse pad. Marty asked her out. They went to plays.

I was too young to understand much about Marty. Mom said he looked like a guy who wore his belt too tight. He kept a mini-vac in his car and vacuumed the interior once or twice a day. He also had a bottle of Windex and a roll of paper towels in the trunk so he could spritz the windows. He drove a Camry, a very middle-of-the-road car.

Mom said she had to break up with him eventually because she couldn't get an image out of her mind. It was the image of Marty, as a small boy, having his shirttail tucked in by his mother. Mom said when she looked at Marty, she pictured an adult woman holding him steady while she shoveled her hand down the back of his pants to get his shirt tucked.

Mom told me that story to explain that you can't pretend your boyfriend is different from what he is. He's not a Ken doll you can dress up. She said sooner or later you're going to see him for what he really is, and you'd better like it when you do.

16

We hung back in the parking lot, waiting for her to show up. The deal was the guy was going to drive her to the motel. Bobby and Pierre had it staked out. Luanne was not supposed to go to any other motel or let him take her anyplace else. I tried to tell them a girl can't always tell a man where she wants to go, but they didn't listen.

Pierre was wicked baked. Bobby, too.

They started to tell me how they'd arranged it with the guy, but I told them I didn't want to know.

The car turned in. An SUV, a Ford.

"That's him, that's him," Pierre whispered, snaky.

They had it worked out that Bobby would stay by the front door, and Pierre would go around the back. They didn't tell me what I should do.

It was late. And the night had a dead feeling to it. No wind. No sound, really.

I stayed next to Bobby and saw Luanne climb out. I looked hard to see if she was okay. She held her coat around her as she got out. The guy climbed out and came around. He had gray hair. He wore a ski parka.

She pulled a key out of her jacket. Opened the door. The guy put his hand on her waist, and they went inside.

"This is horrible," I said to Bobby.

"It's okay, Baby."

I glanced at him. I could tell he didn't like it either. Not now that it was here in front of him.

It was hard to judge time.

I tried to imagine being in that room with that man and it made me shudder to think about it. I wondered if she could go right in, dive into the bathroom, then scramble out the window. Then I wondered where Pierre had parked the car and how was she supposed to get the money anyway. Nothing about it seemed like a good idea.

"You have to go up and knock on the door," I said to Bobby.

He said, "Shhhhh."

"Go," I said. "If you don't, I will."

"They just got there."

"You're stoned, so you don't know shit," I said.

He didn't say anything. He kept watching the door like he expected Tarzan to swing out of a tree.

I shoved him aside and started walking toward the door. The SUV hissed a little as it cooled under the ice. I thought of Luanne in the room, maybe turning to stone. I hurried more, trying to stay calm. Maybe she had already cleared out the window. I didn't want to mess things up, but the timing seemed bad to me.

I knocked on the door and heard something inside.

"Who is it?" a man's voice asked.

"Is my sister in there?" I shouted. It was all I could think to say.

A bunch of scrambling then. He didn't want a loudmouth girl screaming at his door. I knocked again, louder.

"If you don't let me in, I'm calling the cops!" I yelled. "You have an underage woman in there. A girl. You open this door now!"

I was getting slightly hysterical. I was.

The door opened.

Rich people don't get in trouble because they already have money. Poor people get in trouble because they are always trying to figure a way to goose the turkey. That's what my father called it. Goosing the turkey meant trying to turn a turkey into a more elaborate, more expensive bird. I don't know where the phrase came from, and the one time I ate goose meat it tasted like hell. Goosing the turkey, though, that's what poor people do.

Luanne's shirt hung down at her waist. Her bra was pulled off one breast. You could tell she had been in trouble and the man had been groping her.

"She's underage!" I screamed to make him nervous.

He looked about fifty. Long and skinny. He didn't even have his parka off.

"Jesus Christ, I don't know what she is," he said.

"She's my sister and she's fifteen and I'm calling the cops right now," I said.

"You," he said to Luanne, "get out."

She ran past him, her hands pulling her shirt against her. I stood in the doorway.

"You dirty bastard," I said. "You old pervert."

He didn't say anything. He tried to shove the door shut, but my blood was crazy. I wanted to kill him. I stuck my foot in the door and kept it there until Bobby pulled me away.

"That dirty, dirty bastard," I said.

Pierre came sprinting around. He didn't even have a car after all. The whole time, I realized, he had just been planning to have Luanne run out the back way with him. In heels.

I punched him as hard as I could right in the face. He spun but he didn't fall. He wiped blood off his lip but put his arm around Luanne. All concern now. All worry.

Luanne started to laugh.

Bobby gave her a drink of whiskey out of his pocket bottle, and she took two, three pulls as fast as she could. Then she took a step away from all of us and peed. Right there. She peed and you could tell something had broken inside her. She never would have dreamed of doing anything like that before. Bobby looked away. Pierre tried to tell her no, but she kept going anyway.

She started laughing more and more. I thought for a second that this is how people go crazy. They just start to laugh and that's that. It just goes on forever. Little by little, she calmed down. She still cried, but it was a deep, heavy cry. Before, she had seemed like a balloon hissing through the air. Now, she just seemed tired and empty, a paper grocery bag bunched up and ready for popping.

"Are you okay?" Pierre kept asking.

"Obviously she isn't, asshole," I said.

"Screw you," he said to me.

Bobby didn't say anything.

We walked. The cold climbed inside my clothes. I couldn't imagine what Luanne felt like in a short skirt and heels. It was crazy. The whole thing.

I handed out cigarettes. Luanne's hands shook when she got a light from Bobby. Then she asked for more whiskey.

"He didn't even let me go to the bathroom," she said. "He didn't give me a chance."

"What do you mean, wouldn't let you go?" Pierre said.

"Are you stupid?" I asked him. "He wouldn't let her go away from him. That's what she means."

"He started right in," she said.

"For Christ's sakes," Pierre said. "It should have worked." Like he was a genius. Like he was Batman's archenemy and someone had finally defeated his extraordinary calculations.

They had no plan to bring Laika back. A few previous animals had gone up and down, then splashed in the water, but the technology didn't exist to bring Laika back through the atmosphere. She was the only animal deliberately sacrificed by the Russian space program. They had no design to bring her back to earth, so on April 14, 1958, a small bright smear appeared in the night sky of the Northern Hemisphere.

I told Bobby about Nicky, but he didn't really take it in. He listened and nodded. I knew he thought I had overreacted. But all it would take was for Nicky to call home, for Fred and Mary to call Cindy, and that would be that. We wouldn't be hard to find. Burlington wasn't very big.

I told Bobby we needed to get going to Mexico.

"We will," he said. "As soon as I get a stake."

"You mean money?"

He nodded.

His eyes looked blurry and red. He looked older, too, as if he were an insect and had to push into a different stage. It was strange. Pierre had rubbed off on him. That's what it was.

I could tell he wanted to be out, away from talking to me. Wanted to be plotting stupid things with Pierre. I told him to leave.

Luanne came out of the bathroom. She had taken a long shower. She wore a towel around her hair and an old University of Vermont sweatshirt Danny had given her. She had pj bottoms on, too, and for a while she just busied herself straightening the things on her dresser. I didn't want to ask if she was okay. If someone asks if you are okay, it means that person doesn't think the other is okay. I didn't want to do that to her.

I sat on the bed and waited. After a while, she came over and sat with me. She lit a cigarette and handed me one.

"It was fine," Luanne said, blowing smoke at the ceiling. "It was working just the way they set it up, but they hadn't figured on the guy being so horny. He freaking jumped me the minute we shut the door."

"I'm sorry," I said.

"It wasn't any big deal. I mean, nothing happened. The guy just groped me."

"Still," I said.

"I keep thinking what would have happened if you hadn't been there."

I shrugged.

"Bobby and Pierre are idiots," she said. "And I'm an idiot."

"It sounded like a good way to make money."

She stared at me. She took a deep drag.

"They got the hundred bucks," she said. "The guy paid up front. Now they're worried he'll come after them."

"Do you think he will?"

She shrugged.

Danny knocked on the door and then pushed through carrying three bowls of ice cream. He looked shy, but you could tell it was the only thing he could think to do. He carried the tray over to us and let us each take a bowl. Ben and Jerry's Cookie Dough. He took the last bowl off and stood in front of us.

"You guys okay?" he asked.

"Ducky," Luanne said.

And for some reason, that started us all off laughing.

Bobby always said in Mexico you don't need a house or anything else. You can live in a tent right beside the ocean. He said you can work for a small hotel or something, clean dishes, whatever, and live in the sun every day. He said if you can train yourself not to need things, then life becomes simple. It's the needing that complicates things.

Larry and Phil came down and laughed about the whole motel thing. They brought beer and laughed with Pierre and Bobby. Larry and Phil said they told them so. That kind of thing. Men's voices bouncing around the kitchen.

•

Early in the morning snow began to fall. I woke just enough to look out the window. In the early light you could hardly see the flakes, but then the sun grew a little stronger and the flakes took on more definition. I heard Danny snoring. I heard the fridge make ice and spit it into a cup. Someone drove past the house, chains on their tires. I realized the weekend had passed, and Fred and Mary had probably returned from the races. I pictured the snow falling in their meadow, the pine trees bending with the wind. When you look at a sled dog through the snow, running, the shape of the dog's body is the only solid thing. Everything else is white and movement. Just the dog holds a space.

Around nine, I took food out to Laika. Snow almost covered her pole. I played with her, throwing up snowballs that she exploded with a quick bite. I asked her where Sebastian was. She stopped and listened to me, trying to figure what I was asking her. "Sebastian," I repeated.

Then for a time she sat quietly and I petted her. I tried to figure out what I should do next. It felt like something had begun and I didn't know what it was, but it was coming closer. Your life can be changing and you may not even know it. Trying to plan, though, is like reaching a hand in water trying to catch a fish. The refraction makes the fish look closer and farther at the same time. And when you reach your hand in, the fish isn't quite where you thought it would be. You think you can see through the water, but it plays tricks on you. The future is like that. Water. And your hand is down below the surface, grabbing at things.

17

We went to be stone the next morning.

Luanne said that, after a snow, people like getting out, and she was right. Church Street was crowded. We stood on our buckets and put a little snow on our sleeves and head, trying to appear as if the snow had fallen on us. Then at noon, Luanne took me to Arrow's, a piercing and tattoo shop. She told me she wanted to buy me a piercing to thank me for saving her. I got three in my right ear to go with two in my left. She bought me the studs and everything. We hugged afterward.

It got cloudy again that afternoon. Up on the buckets, I kept searching the crowds for signs of Nicky or Cindy or anyone who looked official. Knowing someone might be looking for you can make you paranoid. I couldn't keep my mind on posing or playing with the kids that wandered close. A crowd of Japanese tourists came through, probably on a ski vacation, and they took a bunch of photographs. Each one of them stepped forward, posed with us, kept going. It was strange to think of our pictures, Luanne and mine, in albums over in Japan. Some of them took digital shots, so they could load them onto computers. We would be sent to relatives and business friends, a little caption beside it to explain the picture.

•

When Pierre came through the crowd fast, I knew something had changed.

Here it comes, I thought.

Watching him come closer was like watching someone move her hand in just a way that you knew she would knock a glass off a counter. You could see it coming, and you knew it was going to be a shame, but it all seemed predestined. Pierre's coming closer felt like that. His face appeared tight and worried. And you saw that he hurried but that his hurrying wasn't going to change anything. I felt a knot in the center of my stomach. Luanne saw him, too. She stood up straight and looked at him. We watched him come forward, a little pinball bouncing off people.

"Bobby just got arrested," Pierre said before he even reached us. "They just took him."

"For what?" Luanne asked.

Pierre put his finger to his nose, pretended to inhale.

Coke.

And probably E.

I didn't move. I pretended to be stone and it worked a little.

My head did the calculations.

1. Bobby wasn't going to foster care.
2. Bobby wasn't going to get away.
3. Bobby was going to prison.
4. I couldn't go near Bobby, or they would take me in, too.
5. Bobby had run out of chances.

6. I wasn't going to Mexico.
7. Bobby wasn't going to Mexico.
8. Maybe we never had a chance of going to Mexico.
9. Maybe it had all been talk and air.
10. If Bobby hadn't met Pierre, he would have met someone else to get him in trouble.
11. Bobby had been heading toward trouble since I met him.
12. Bobby wouldn't tell the police where he lived, but Cindy might read the report of his arrest and put two and two together.
13. I had no place to go and no one to go with.
14. I had to leave.

What happened was this: Bobby had been selling pot next to the dolphin fountain at the start of Church Street. If he wanted something harder, some E or coke, he told Pierre, then Pierre got it from his stash. They had walkie-talkies so they could communicate. They had a code all set up. E was Ed. Coke was Connie. Stupid stuff like that. They thought they were slicker than any cops could be.

So a kid came up and wanted to buy something. E, coke. A friend of a friend. He knew Bobby's name. Bobby said he didn't know what the kid was talking about. Then Bobby asked him if he was a cop. That's what you're supposed to do. The guy has to admit to being a cop if you ask. But technically the guy wasn't a cop, so he said no. Then Bobby called Pierre, said he needed some stuff. Pierre handed it off and Bobby sold it. Three cops zoomed right down on him as he made the transaction. Set up all the way. They threw him down on the ground and cuffed him. People stood around and made laughing noises. They pushed his face into the snow, Pierre said. And when Bobby stood up, the snow stuck there, like his cheek had turned to cement.

Pierre watched it from a block away. He beat feet as soon as he saw what was going down. Now he doesn't know if he should stay in the area. He figures they might want him next. Or that Bobby might say something. He says when someone is drowning, they'll grab anything to save themselves. You never know. It's the only smart thing Pierre has ever said.

Laika's heart rate rose to triple its normal rate, the Russian scientist admitted. She had been in the capsule for four days. The g forces and the noise must have terrified her. Originally, the Russian news agencies contended that she had lived four or five days. But more recent revelations concluded she died shortly after entering orbit. Her entire flight lasted 162 days, but she probably lived for only a few hours. Her life signs failed. *Sputnik II* drifted through space, the quiet dog down in its belly.

Luanne and Danny drove me. I sat in back with Laika, watching the snow and the dark countryside pass. I didn't know the exact route to Fred and Mary's, but Danny helped me by getting an atlas. Then he called their phone number and pretended to be a UPS driver who needed help delivering a package. He got their street number and directions to their house.

We ate at a bowling alley. Danny insisted we play a few games, so we did. Danny wanted to play, I figured, because he was pretty good. Surprisingly good. He was a big guy who looked a little like

Fred Flintstone twinkle-toeing up to the foul line. He bowled a 140 or so. Luanne and I didn't do better than a 50.

It was nice, though. The lanes weren't crowded, and we drank cherry Cokes. Danny ordered a lot of food as a going-away present to me. They made wicked good fries, and we scarfed them down. Then the bowling ball got greasy and salty and slipped out of our hands. We laughed pretty hard. It felt like something was breaking up, but it was okay. We watched the bowlers, these guys who took it seriously, and it cracked us up. The guys held the balls up in front of them and stared down the alleys. They looked like praying mantises that had just caught black beetles.

Luanne put coins in the jukebox, and we got to listen to a few of our songs. Midway through our last game, the night turned into disco bowl, which made the whole thing even funnier. They shut off the lights and ran a strobe over everything. Disco queens of the bowling alley. Luanne and I danced like crazy. Danny sat watching, his fingers finding food, his head popping to the music.

In the back of the car, I thought of Bobby in a prison suit. A jumpsuit, gray, and flip-flops. They give you baking soda for toothpaste and a single comb. I knew Bobby would be scared, but he would pretend not to be. I pictured him touching the front of his hair, the way he does, and twirling it when he's nervous.

If you sit and look out the rear window long enough, and it's dark outside, you can get confused whether the car is moving or if maybe the land has decided to ripple away and you are seeing the earth spinning while you sit perfectly still and watch.

•

They dropped me at eleven o'clock. I made them pull past the house, down the road about a half mile, and we sat for a while.

"You sure?" Luanne asked me.

"I'm not sure of anything," I said.

"It's for the best," Danny said. "Give you a chance to get on your feet."

"She's on her feet," Luanne said. "Don't talk a lot of shit, Danny."

"You know what I mean," he said.

I hugged them. Then I took Laika's leash and climbed out. She jumped down after me. The car pulled away slowly, its taillights red and glowing in the exhaust. I felt more alone than I had ever felt in my life.

When Laika smelled the dogs, she pulled. And the dogs began to bark. At first they made whining sounds only, but then they caught our scent. Then one of them began to turn the barks into a howl, and the others joined in. Laika heard the sound and couldn't contain it. She danced around me. Too excited to howl. The dogs' voices continued to blend until it became a siren, one sound, a pole of noise on a winter night.

We skirted the trees, following the same route Bobby had used to get us. The house lights were extinguished, but a cotton string of smoke pushed out of the chimney. I let Laika pull me. I felt tired and cold. Snow clogged my steps, and beyond the pines we had to go slowly, Laika porpoising while I took slow strides. Peg-holing. Snow went down my shoes, up my pant legs. The studs on my ears turned

sciously grip the shovel. *Here are my fingers*, I told myself. Now I have to bend them. I dug a little dog poo and threw it in the manure pile. A little more. I didn't feel any warmer.

"Did you know Laika was the name of the first space dog?" I asked Fred.

He stopped what he was doing. Looked at me. Nodded.

Then he went back to work.

We worked for ten or fifteen minutes that way. He didn't say anything else. I couldn't tell if he was angry or glad to see me. Fred does what's in front of him.

When he finished with the other dogs, he went inside the kennel and examined Laika. She jumped and spun around, but he settled her eventually. He inspected her paws, her eyes and ears, her belly. He ran his fingers over her ribs.

"You took good care of her," he said. "She's none the worse for wear."

"I wouldn't let anything happen to her."

"I knew that," he said. "I counted on that."

If you make a habit of making movie moments, I wonder if they can become real. I wonder if all of life isn't just making up your own movie.

Mary looked me up and down.

"Look at the new dog I found in one of the barrels," Fred said. "She's a friend of Laika's."

"You hungry?" Mary asked.

I nodded.

"Maybe you ought to grab a quick shower," she said. "You know where it is."

I nodded again.

"We'll call Cindy while you're showering," Mary said. "You should know what's what. No secrets."

"I understand," I said.

She started to say something, then bit her lip.

I went and got in the shower. I stayed in it a long time. I started thinking about Bobby, and my mom, and even my dad, and I cried into a washcloth. I thought of Danny, too, thought of how he would never get thin, never be able to be at peace with that, and that thought got me crying harder. Mixed in was a lot of self-pity, a feeling that I hadn't anyplace to go or be, and that made me even sadder. It felt like I had a sponge inside me that had to be wrung out and made absorbent again. It sounds funny, I know, but that's what it felt like.

When I dried myself, I could see in the mirror the tiger stripes of the tattoo spelling out Bobby.

I dressed and went to breakfast. Mary had oatmeal and melon and fresh bread. Fred had gone out to cut down a birch that had snapped in the last storm. He probably wanted to give us some time to talk. Sebastian went with him. I ate a lot. Mary waited until I had a cup of tea in front of me before she told me what Cindy had to say.

"She's relieved you're okay," she said. "That's the first thing."

I nodded.

"And she's angry with you. So am I. I won't speak for Fred, but he wasn't happy, I can tell you. Not when he found you took Laika."

"I didn't mean to," I said.

"We mean to do what we do," Mary said. "That's just logic."

I nodded. Still chewing on it.

"Your boyfriend is arrested and is going to do two to five years in prison," she said. "Cindy wanted you to know. By the time he gets out, he will be over twenty-one years old. He's not eligible for parole or anything else for quite a while. You'll be eighteen, maybe older."

I nodded.

"She wants to talk to you later, but she wanted me to tell you that, so you would know. She knew you were in Burlington. Nicky said he spotted you."

Again, I nodded.

"Cindy has to check some things in the office. It's still early. She asked if we wanted you to stay with us."

"What did you say?" I asked.

She looked at me. It might have been a movie moment, but she looked me straight in the eye. "I said we wanted you here," she said. "That goes for both of us."

I nodded and drank some tea. It tasted like mint.

When the Russians built a statue to commemorate the early pioneers of their space program, they included a small dog, down by the legs of the cosmonauts, looking out quietly. Laika. She was a part-Samoyed terrier. Her name, in Russian, means "Little Curly," just as Wally said.

"Until we know what's going to happen to you, you can at least help around here," Mary said. "Come into the kitchen and help me straighten up."

We carried the breakfast things in and put them to soak. Mary stationed me at the sink, washing and rinsing, while she stashed food away. She clicked on the radio and we listened to National Public Radio. A guy gave the weather report. Cold and snowy. Another guy read a report about a new wheelchair someone invented. Then a woman in Maine read a story she had written about her antique chickens. The woman raised breeds that had gone out of favor. Old breeds. European breeds. She was bringing them back. One of her chickens laid blue eggs.

It was nice in the kitchen. I liked the sounds of the plates clicking and knocking together, and the noise the silverware made scraping things. Mary came beside me and loaded what I had rinsed into the dishwasher. Now and then she went to the side window to check on Fred. She worried the tree might spring and jump, bent and twisted as it was by the storm. A widow maker, she called it. A tree that could kill a man.

But eventually she heard the tree fall. And Fred waved to her. He knew she watched and worried. I realized that counted for something, maybe counted for everything.

I wiped down the counters and the stove. Mary cleaned the coffeepot. By the time we finished, everything was stowed and shipshape. The dishwasher made a nice, steady hum. I felt warm and tired.

Mary asked kind of sideways, without really looking at me, "Are you using a lot of drugs, Baby?"

I shook my head. No.

"I'll take your word," she said.

I looked at her.

"May I lay down for a while?" I asked. I felt like I might put my head down on the kitchen counter and fall asleep.

She nodded.

"Go ahead," she said. "I'll wake you when Cindy calls."

"Thank you," I said.

"You know, Baby," she said, "life doesn't have to be this hard. It can be easier than you're making it."

"I'm trying to learn that."

"There's no such thing as trying," Mary said. "There's only doing and not doing."

Wind outside. A down comforter. A cold window. Sebastian snoring beside the bed. Wool socks. Clean hair. The sound of voices in the next room. Quiet voices. Worn jeans. Detergent smell on the sheets. Trees rocking back and forth. The sun low and soft and not interested this day. Barn boards. A roof beam. The clock marking time in the dining room.

"A friend of mine, another social worker, he saw Bobby. Bobby's over eighteen, so that makes him legally an adult. He's in a pickle," Cindy said over the phone.

"Is he all right?"

"Define all right," Cindy said.

"Is he depressed?"

"I suppose so. I understand your concern, but Bobby's not really my problem right now," Cindy said.

"Bobby's not a problem," I said. "The legal system is the problem."

"Maybe you're right. I don't know. I can't change the whole world."

"People sell weapons all the time. America does. We sell weapons all over the world, but a kid sells a little pot and he gets put away."

"Again," Cindy said, "I appreciate your point of view. I'm even glad you have a political opinion. But Bobby's situation is not my chief concern right now. I'll tell you what I'll do. If you stay in touch, I promise I will stay in touch with my friend. Bobby's caseworker. And eventually you can talk to Bobby yourself. Fair enough?"

"Okay," I said.

"In return, you have to do me one other favor," she said. "You have to promise that you won't build Bobby up in your head. Turn him into a rebel outlaw. He's just a kid without many resources who got caught doing something stupid."

"Screw you," I said. "You don't know Bobby."

"The truth is the truth, Baby. Bobby is not going to like the next couple years. That's just a fact."

I didn't say anything.

Sebastian sat beside me under the wall phone. I had my hand on his big head. It was late morning, and the sky still glimmered gray and quiet. The dogs barked. Fred had gone out there, but he wouldn't be long. He had talked about taking a training run in the afternoon. Mary had given me the phone and went back into the house somewhere.

"Let's talk about you for a few minutes," Cindy said. "Do you think you can stay at the Potters for a while? Can we trust you to stay?"

I didn't say anything.

Cindy said, "Because they won't take you back the next time. That's the deal. They have other things they can be doing."

"I'm not a thing," I said.

"I mean the time they spend with you, if you don't want it, can be spent on someone else. Don't play lawyer with me, Baby."

"I hate all this shit," I said.

"What shit would that be?"

"This negotiation about my time, and where I am."

"You came back to the Potters. That tells me something."

"Cindy, get a life."

She laughed.

Sebastian shifted to get my hand moving on his head again.

"Okay, here's the deal. Stay at the Potters at least until racing season is over. You like the dogs, Baby, and don't say you don't. I'm working on a few things from my end. You're fifteen, so letting you fly free is not an option. If you decide to run away, there's not a lot we can do, Baby. In three years you'll be a legal adult and then no one can interfere with anything you want to do. I know that seems like a long wait, but it will go by quickly."

I didn't say anything.

"Let's not forget, though, that you have a few charges in your background," Cindy said. "Legal issues. The court expects decent behavior out of you."

"Whatever," I said.

"Good behavior is like a big eraser. It will help you just wipe out the past."

"I don't want to wipe out my past," I said.

"You know what I mean," she said.

"I'll stay at the Potters," I said.

"Good. I'll work on things from my end. And I will call you with a way to speak to Bobby. Can I say one other thing?"

I didn't say anything.

"You're not going to be fifteen forever, Baby. You can like the flowers right now, but you have to plant some vegetables, too."

"That's daft," I said.

She laughed again.

"I mean, you have to enjoy the moment, but the smart person also plans for the future. Your future is coming fast, Baby. Your mother modeled a pattern for you of running away from things. Sorry, but that's true. So ask yourself, if you get itchy to leave or go somewhere, whether you aren't just living out a pattern your mother set out for you."

"Thank you, Oprah."

She laughed.

Then she hung up.

In New York City, in Central Park, there is a statue of Balto. Balto is famous as the dog that helped transport medicine during a diphtheria epidemic in Nome, Alaska. The story is well known. When Balto led his team back to Nome, carrying the medicine with him, he became the most renowned dog in the world. Disney eventually made a movie about him, and Steven Spielberg produced it. The Iditarod is a race run in memory of the diphtheria outbreak and of the dogs that brought the medicine. Racers travel through the same towns—Solomon, Golovin, Kuyuk, Elim, Unalakleet, Shaktoolik—as the dogs did in 1925.

Most people never heard of Togo, another sled dog. But Togo was the greatest lead dog ever. It was Togo who ran nine-tenths of the dash for the medicine. Togo led the driver, Leonhard Seppala, and his team across the sea ice, an incredibly perilous journey, and brought them back safely. He never quit. He ran his heart, as drivers say. But leading a team is so exhausting that he ruined himself. He was spent; he had given too much of himself.

Another team brought the medicine to Nome. One of Togo's kennel mates, Balto, led over the final fifty miles. When the team that ran only fifty of the four hundred miles entered the city, Balto became world-famous.

Togo lived quietly the rest of his life and never raced again.

19

"Three ... , two ... , one ... , go, driver!"

"Up Charlie, up Willow, up! Go go go go go!"

The streak of spectators flashed by and then we banked left, softly spraying snow behind us. The weather snapped sharp and sweet. A cold day. A cloudy day. We ran down the first hill, up the second. In no time we caught the team in front of us, a frumpy team made of hodge-podge dogs, a woman named Sparrow on the sled. Sparrow yelled at her dogs in a high-pitched squeak, birdlike, but we shot past her, beautiful Charlie pulling her heart out, Willow graceful and tongue-lagging. Second Boss and Muppin dug in and yanked and we went past, two trains side by side, one going faster. I saw Sparrow wave, and she whooped at our speed and yelled, "Go get them," because I was a woman, a female, and we were kicking ass.

Run, you beautiful dogs. You Second Boss. You Muppin. You Teddy and Rocky. As I love you, as you love me. Run, my darlings, my darling dogs.

Then we clicked down a beech hill, all brown leaves fluttering on either side of us, and I felt comfortable and solid. Air came into my lungs and out. Breathe. Frost started to cover my cheeks and brows, but I didn't care. We ran through the woods in Maine, dark clouds above, and I pumped to keep the sled gliding right, pumped to help them, felt like a dog myself, one big dog and the wind straight in my face.

"Haw over!" I yelled.

And we went left.

I had to brake around a sharp turn and a runner went up on a bump, nearly tossed me, but I held on. Then another bump came faster than I knew and I fell, one knee smacking *whack* on a rock. Pain ran up me like a river but I held, kicked at the snow, let the dogs' speed spin me to my feet. Charlie ran her heart. And Willow ran and Second Boss, heavy and true, leaned into the traces and kept them tight. And a gray spin of sky above, pines, pines, and then snow and nothing but ice and the lake.

Another team. Black dogs. Robert something-or-other, a mean man, ugly, who shook chains at the dogs to scare them. Fred hated him and I hated him for Fred. But his team was good and we ran like nuts going after them, bending out around an island in the center of the lake. A wind pulled a rooster tail off the ice and snow, and for a second it was impossible to sense movement at all. We ran inside a snow globe, all of us, and nothing existed except the dogs in front of us and a sense that the wind might never quiet. But it did and the snow dropped and we had gained on Robert's team. I heard him shake his chains, saw his dogs pull harder, but now Charlie saw them. And what she saw passed to the rest of the team and I felt a spinal shiver run down through them.

"Take us home, Charlie!" I yelled.

Nothing could stop her. Nothing could hold against her. She ran like a hot demon, and Willow strained to stay beside her. The wheel dogs, Muppin and Second Boss, gave her everything. Claw and teeth and tongue and snow, ground passing, sky, trees, and we were on them.

"Trail!" I shouted.

Into your heart, Robert. I see into your heart and you cannot match the hearts of my dogs and their joy at running. This joy will beat your dogs and you know it, fear loses to joy, and that's all you will get of my dogs.

"On by, Charlie!" I yelled. "On by, Willow!"

He did not yield. His lead dog snapped at Charlie.

"Get off my dogs!" I screamed. "Don't you touch a hair on my dogs! Trail, you jerk!"

We went by.

I cut out his heart and fed it to my dogs.

"Home, Charlie, bring us home."

We went along the lake. Robert's team faded. I turned on the sled runners and watched him fall behind. Then we were in the lead, the finest team in the six-dog division, the purest, the sweetest. We ran our hearts and glided. Willow's tongue slopped along and for a second stuck to the brass clip of her neckline. When she pulled it free, a circle of blood dripped on the snow. I told her it was okay. I told her she would get extra food. I sang to Charlie to bring us home.

We were not far from shore when the ice began to break.

It was tested, they said later.

Snowmobiles had been over it, they said later.

It was a foot thick, three feet in places.

Everyone agreed it had no business failing.

But Charlie started to skid, and I heard a crack like a pool shot snapping around me. And suddenly we compressed, an accordion crushing, the whole team skidding to a stop and the ice, unsure, supported us still. I had no time to think. I applied the brake, but it was too late and Charlie went through and Willow beside her. Then like pearls slipping off the edge of a dressing table, the other dogs followed them under. They braced their legs, but there was nothing to hold them. Ice became water by magic beneath their paws. Then the sled tilted. Then I hit the cold.

20

I fell forward. The momentum carried me.

The sled sank headfirst, sounding, and I followed it.

The handle struck my chest. Or I slammed against it. But I had a vision that the dogs still ran, down deep, down under the water, we ran until the earth opened beneath us and a great white breath greeted us. All the dogs in the world waited for us. We ran down deeper and deeper, and the dogs ran as never before. And I dreamed we would never want, never cry, and that Charlie had brought us home at last.

My jacket sucked water and wrapped around me. My gloves, too. I saw disconnected details. Pines. A blue jay making a sound like wire. The bottom of the ice. The sled, floating like kelp.

Cold.

Great cold. That was the next sensation. The cold filled me, and nothing mattered except the cold. I had no sense of the dogs. It took a moment to realize I was under the dogs, that I could see their legs yanking, trying to run. Air had left my lungs. I had followed the sled down, and now it was time to rise.

I saw Charlie sink, then go up, then sink again.

Then I understood.

I pushed up. I pulled through the water, through the gangline, and came to the surface. Then the world became real again, genuine, and I came through the skim ice and found myself in the middle of the team, the dogs furious around me.

"It's okay," I shouted to them. "It's okay."

But it wasn't.

My mind did the quick calculations. The sled anchored them. They had no chance of swimming, no chance of staying above water as long as the sled held them. We were not far from shore. I could see the shoreline, the green frown of trees, the trail leading to the finish.

I stood.

My feet found the bottom.

That was the first step. That was a big thing to know. I could stand. The dogs could not, but I could.

I bit the toe of my right glove and pulled my hand free. I found the gangline and ran my fingers up it until I found Second Boss's neckline. I unhooked it. Then I unhooked his tailline and he swam free.

"Go," I told him.

He did. Then I found Teddy and Rocky's line. And Muppin's. But it was all a tangle and I had to pull myself along the line. Each time the dogs surged they yanked the line out of my hands. And my hands did not work well. The cold had taken my fingers and turned them into Popsicles. They felt thick and useless. It took me a long time to release Muppin. I stared at him as he finally shook free. His face looked still. I couldn't be certain he was still alive, but he swam after Second Boss. I saw them shake on shore.

Charlie was not above the surface.

And neither was Willow.

I heard a bullhorn squawk. Then I heard snowmobiles. Someone was coming to help, maybe lots of people, but right now they were on land and I was not and the dogs could not wait for them.

I forced my fingers back to the gangline. Something wrapped around my wrist and yanked me down. I nearly went off my feet. Then I thought of the dogs pulling me, a great weighted balloon, behind the sled. Then I thought of Luanne and how this was the way to turn to stone. Water could turn you to stone if it was cold enough. She needed to know that.

Everything went slower.

I pushed past Teddy and Rocky. I yanked at the gangline. Charlie rose up and Willow, too, but I could not tell if they were alive. I decided then to become a tree. To be pure stone. I stood in the middle of the four dogs, Charlie and Willow in front, Rocky and Teddy behind, and pulled the gangline over my shoulders. My fingers failed. I could no longer manipulate anything, but I could be vertical. I could be what the dogs could not be for themselves. I stood and gathered the dogs in my arms. Their claws raked at my legs and they could not contain their panic, but I kept all four dogs' heads above water. That was all I could do. I stood facing out to the lake, and the rooster tails of snow and ice still lifted but I did not care. I held the dogs. Then behind me I heard shouting and heard the bullhorn again, and then splashing. Someone was coming. I could not bring myself to look at Charlie. I could not look at her. I cradled her closer to me and stood straighter, taller, keeping them free of the water. The cold locked us together. Ice tried to form around us, but I was only chest deep, not too bad, and the dogs' struggles kept the water moving.

I thought of Laika, up in space, the cold capsule spinning forever and ever until it hit the atmosphere. A shooting star. A brush of light on a spring night.

Greg, the club president, reached me first.

His hands released the dogs. And he lifted them and threw them toward shore. I could not tell if the dogs swam or merely skimmed across the surface.

He released them in order, working up the gangline toward me. Then he grabbed me.

"Are you okay?" he shouted.

Everything seemed like a shout.

I nodded.

Then more men were in the water beside me. And I felt myself float up and go toward shore. Someone carried a dog. Someone carried my arms, and someone carried my legs. I heard a siren, and I heard more snowmobiles. Suddenly the pines stood right above me, and someone bent over me. I heard them pulling the sled up. It came out of the water and made a sloshing sound. Someone debated about taking off my clothes. They didn't know if the clothes protected me or drew more heat from my body, but then a paramedic arrived. I knew she was a paramedic by her hat.

Are the dogs okay? I wanted to ask.

But I could not open my mouth. Ice had closed it.

A human can die in minutes in freezing water.

Hypothermia.

If you are hiking in the woods, and you begin to lose your body heat, you become confused. You cannot tell a good decision from a poor one. Soon you wander and get colder, and soon you die. You die shaking, the final bit of heat in your system evaporating like rain on summer tar.

I do not remember:

1. The ambulance ride.
2. Them undressing me.
3. Fred or Mary.
4. The doctors.

I do remember:

1. Pins and needles in my limbs. Like an electric current.
2. My hair frozen to my hat.
3. My pants too frozen to permit my legs to bend.
4. Sirens, the *whoop whoop whoopdedededede* kind.
5. Madonna singing "Like a Virgin" on a radio.
6. My tattoo hurting, but I don't know why.
7. My nose and ear studs cold as bullets. Dead stars.
8. A hot liquid burning my tongue as it went down.

I woke at night.

Mary sat beside my bed. She had a book open on her lap.

We looked at each other for a long time.

Then I went back to sleep.

•

"No, you're not, Bobby."

"I'm in prison," he said, and laughed.

We didn't speak for a second. Then he said he had to go. People were lined up behind him to use the phone.

"Are you okay, Bobby?" I asked.

"I'm okay."

"You're not a loser, Bobby. You're not."

"Okay," he said.

He hung up. I hung up after him.

Bobby would have stayed with the dogs and done the same as I did. I would bet my life on it.

21

I went with Fred and Sebastian down to the kennels. It was a comparatively warm day—maybe twenty-five degrees. It was my first day back, my first time to see the dogs since the ice. I felt good. My legs still wobbled a little, but otherwise I was back to normal.

I started to tear up when I saw the dogs. They bounced up against the kennel fences, their paws holding onto the grid. Second Boss, Willow, Rocky, Muppin, Teddy Roosevelt, Charlie. I opened the door to Charlie's kennel and went inside. I knelt next to her and held her against me. She felt dry and warm. I put my face in her fur, trying to feel the heat from sunlight stored there.

Fred stood outside the kennel.

"You know," he said, "I'm not sure I ever said how much I admired what you did that day."

I nodded, my face still on Charlie's back.

"All your life," Fred said, "you'll know you did a courageous thing. That's wonderful to know about yourself."

I nodded.

"Want to run them?" Fred asked.

I nodded again.

•

When we had them lined out, Fred put Laika in Willow's place at lead.

"Mary and I talked," Fred said. "Laika's your dog."

I looked at him.

Then I pulled the quick release that anchored us to the tie-out pole. And we took off.

Down through the woods. Laika was not as fast as Willow, not at first, but she found her pace and Charlie insisted she stay beside her. We took a long sweeping right turn, a gee over, and then straightened. I let them go easy. They had not run since the ice, and there was no rush. I watched them for signs of hesitation, worry, but they seemed fine. Fred had plans to run them on a lake before the next race, I knew, but today it was only woods and a calm training run. They smoothed along, running gracefully. Laika ran at the lead, her neckline even with Charlie's.

When I reached the middle of the run, just before we turned for home, I braked the sled and planted the snow hook. The dogs slowed and stopped. I hopped off the runners and walked up through the team. I petted them all and then fell on my knees beside Laika. I held her. Her head rested over my shoulders, her eyes looking down the trail.

The ice taught me you can't know the future. You never can. What looks like ice can be simply water holding snow.

Luanne stepped inside the house.

"It's beautiful," she whispered.

We hugged. We stood for a second in the doorway, looking at each other.

"Are you sure it's okay?" she asked.

"They said it was fine. They want to meet you. Don't worry about anything. They're nice people."

I walked Luanne into the keeping room. That's what Fred and Mary called the room with the woodstove. Luanne wore a hippie skirt—her idea of dressing up—and a baggy sweater. But she had pulled her hair back. She looked good, if skinny.

Fred stood when she entered.

"This is Luanne, Fred," I said.

They shook hands.

"The gargoyle," he said.

Luanne's face went white a little, but she saw Fred had been joking.

"Yes," she said. "I guess I am."

Mary came up from downstairs carrying laundry.

"Great to meet you," she said when I introduced her to Luanne. "I hope you'll stay to dinner."

"I don't know … ," Luanne said, looking at me.

"Sure she'll stay," I said.

I took her by the hand and led her to my room.

For a moment we felt awkward. I didn't know how she felt exactly, but it was weird to see her away from Burlington, away from her house, from the gargoyle suits. She seemed nervous. I figured maybe she was reliving some of her own foster parent experiences. It probably weirded her out.

I told her to sit on my bed and tell me everything, and that seemed to give her something to do. She told me Danny had met a girl, believe it or not, and he was trying to lose weight. He liked her a lot. Her name was Daphne, which was a weird name, and it was weirder, too, to have Danny and Daphne. D & D. A couple. But Danny was still sweet. His parents were helping him buy a limousine. He was thinking of trying that as a business. They had this big family plan to help Danny by putting him into a car. Luanne didn't think it would work.

Pierre was Pierre. No one had caught him. No one had done anything to him. He was still dealing. He was an ass. He hadn't even visited Bobby. Not once. He hung out with Larry and Phil, although Larry was having trouble with child custody and that kind of crap. Larry was somebody's daddy, and that was hard to believe.

Luanne said she had been doing yoga. Eating well. Behaving. She had been a gargoyle every day for two weeks straight. Tips came in better with the warmer weather. She had applied for a hawkers' and peddlers' license so she could be legitimate. She said if I ever wanted to join her and become a second gargoyle to let her know.

Then she looked at me and said, "But you stay here, Baby, as long as you can. Don't mess this. I don't mean for you to come and join me. Don't mess this."

"I won't," I said.

"Promise me. Not for Bobby or for anyone."

"I promise," I said.

I took her out in the afternoon to meet all the dogs. I gave her one of the Potters' mackinaws to wear. She looked funny in her hippie skirt and big coat, but she liked the dogs. She squatted next to Laika to say hello. Then she reached through the grid to pet the others. She especially liked Earth Monkey, one of the dogs on Fred's team.

"They're beautiful," she said, her face down to meet them. "Aren't you, guys?"

"You should see them run. They just go."

"You can drive a dogsled, Baby. I still can't believe that."

"Neither can I."

"I mean," she said, "you never think someone you know will do stuff like that. You know what I mean? I don't know how to explain it. Like if you hear someone sailed around the world. You just realize one day they pushed off from the dock and went. I doubt I'm making any sense."

"I think I know what you mean," I said.

We let Laika out. She sniffed Luanne for a while before she spotted Sebastian coming out of the house. When she saw the big dog, she sprinted off to greet him. Luanne and I watched her run. She threw her front legs through her back legs, ran at the sun as if to keep it from falling out of sight.

We had onion soup, French bread, and a salad for dinner. Mary poured us each a glass of wine. Luanne looked at me. I gave her a small nod that it was okay to drink the wine. Sebastian sat beside her, his head as tall as the table. Luanne's face looked healthy from being outdoors.

"We have a race this weekend," Fred said to her. "You would be welcome to join us or at least ride up for the day. It's not far from Burlington."

"Please do," Mary said.

"I'll try to," Luanne said.

She glanced at me. Quick. She wasn't accustomed to adults inviting her places.

"Tell me about being a gargoyle," Mary said. "I'm intrigued, I have to admit."

"There's not much to it," Luanne said.

Mary passed around more bread and said, "I'm sure there's some trick to it. There's a trick to almost everything."

You could tell Mary wanted to draw Luanne out but only in a good way.

"Well," Luanne said, "this sounds crazy, but I always think of being on a wall and water comes out of my mouth."

Fred laughed.

"That's the trick then," he said.

"I read," she said, going on, "that gargoyles represented pagan religions. So when they built cathedrals like Notre Dame, the gargoyles served to unite earlier beliefs with the new Christian ones. That's what I read, anyway. I've told this so many times that Baby is probably sick of hearing about it."

"Fascinating," Mary said. "You've taught me something."

Luanne shrugged.

And the phone rang.

Usually Fred and Mary did not answer the phone during a meal. They usually let the answering machine pick it up.

But they must have known something was up. Mary stood, excused herself, and went into the kitchen.

And just by the silence after she said hello, you knew something important had happened. I wondered if something had happened to Nicky. I looked at Fred. He had his spoon suspended between his mouth and the onion soup. A piece of cheese dangled from the spoon. Luanne picked up the vibe. She reached forward and broke off a piece of bread.

Mary returned a minute later. She snatched up her napkin and sat back down.

Calmly, she looked at me. "Seems Cindy has found your mother" was all Mary said.

Fred told me a French phrase to keep in mind when I thought of my mother.

Tout comprendre, tout pardonner.

Translated, it means, "All understood, all forgiven."

Fred says if we could know, honestly know, exactly why anyone does something, then we would be obliged to forgive her or him. Everyone is worthy of forgiveness. Even a serial killer. If you could go back far enough into their lives, into their DNA, you could figure out why they killed people. No one, Fred says, grows up and says, "Gee, I'd like to become a serial killer." They become one because they grow to a certain sun we may never see or comprehend. But if we do understand it, then we must forgive, because how else could they have grown?

"She's an alcoholic, Baby," Cindy said on the phone. "You should know that going into it. She was picked up on a disorderly. That's how we tracked her down."

"When?"

"About a week ago. She had been down in Texas, I guess. She moved back here. She said part of the reason she moved up here was to find you. You can take that however you want. I'm just reporting the little I know."

I looked out the window. It was dark. Luanne had gone.

"Have you talked to her?"

"No," Cindy said. "My colleague in Massachusetts dinged her on the computer. Routine checking. Honestly, we didn't expect to find her. He talked to her briefly."

"But she didn't contact you?"

"No, Baby, she didn't."

I took a deep breath. Laika slept at the foot of my bed. I put my foot on her belly and rubbed softly. She uncurled a bit to give me better access. But she didn't wake.

"What are my options?"

"We have to take it slow. My colleague—a guy named Steve—is going over to see her tomorrow. He's going to assess the situation. See if she seems stable. He'll talk with her. There are a lot of conditions that have to be met."

"Like what?"

"Well, we have to see what men might be around. That kind of thing. We don't want to introduce you into a difficult environment. Can she care for you? Does she have a means of income? That sort of thing."

"I want to see her."

"I know you do," Cindy said. "I understand."

"Even if I can't stay there, I need to see her. That's my feeling."

"That's natural. I'll do everything I can to make sure that happens."

"Is she married?"

"I don't know."

"Where did she get arrested? Did she get arrested?"

"Yes, just held for her own safety. A bar in Massachusetts outside of Boston. I guess it's kind of a biker place. You know."

"I know," I said.

"Little by little. Just be encouraged that we know where she is. And she's alive. I'm trying to walk a thin line here with you, Baby. I don't want to set you up for disappointment, and I don't want to come across as a wet blanket. I'm trying to stay neutral, sort of, though I'm on your side."

I didn't say anything.

"I know it will be hard, but this is a time to depend on your head more than your heart. You have to be a little cautious. That's hard right now, I know. Very hard. Your mother is complicated, Baby. The whole situation is complicated. You know anything about boxing? Well, keep your hands up so you don't get clobbered. You know what I mean?"

"I guess so."

"I promise we'll move on it as quickly as possible. I understand how important this is for you. I hesitated even telling you until we had the full picture, but I thought you deserved to know. It's your mom, your family."

"Thank you."

For a second she didn't say anything. The phone hiss went in and out.

"Mary and Fred know the situation," she said a moment later. "You can count on them to be steady. They will follow your lead. And, Baby, you know it won't do any good to go rushing off anyplace. Please tell me you understand that."

"I do."

"Just hold tight a little longer. We'll see what happens. I'll call you as soon as I know anything."

"When will your friend see her?"

"Tomorrow morning, first thing. He put it at the top of his list."

"Thank you," I said.

"It's what I do," she said.

22

During the night a wind came and broke three windowpanes in the dining room. Fred and Mary speculated what it might have been. If the windows had broken during the day, then they would have thought a bird had been blown through. But three birds? All at once? Fred climbed a ladder and perched there a while. He used cardboard and duct tape to close the holes. The wind played through the holes like air going through bagpipes.

It gave the morning an odd quiet. Listening, you expected wind and were disappointed when it didn't come. The woodstove burned and fluttered with the wind up in its stack. After Fred finished with the window, he carried in three armfuls of firewood from the woodshed. I helped him.

"Did you hear the banshee last night?" Fred asked as we dumped the wood by the stove.

"What banshee?"

"Why, the north spirit from Ireland. If you hear her, you will lead a charmed life."

"I'm charmed all right," I said.

It was only seven o'clock. I knew Fred was trying to distract me. He put me to work mucking out the kennels. Then we changed runners on the sled. Fred had me help him administer worm medicine to the dogs. They licked their chops and looked like children swallowing something disagreeable.

Then we fussed around with harnesses, checking to see that the kennels were in good order. Fred was not the sort to let things become untidy, so there wasn't much point to it. When we finished, we wandered back inside. I brought Laika with me. Mary had gone to the grocery store. She also had some books to drop off at the library.

It was nearly nine o'clock.

I went in the bathroom and took off all my studs.

The nose stud. The ear studs.

I stared a long time in the mirror. My skin appeared naked. Small white dots marked where the studs had blocked the sun.

I took a hot shower afterward. When I came out, no one had called.

The Ponte della Maddalena, a bridge in Italy's Tuscany province, is also known as the Devil's Bridge. It is a beautiful bridge, and legend holds that the builder, seeing its potential beauty but unable to complete it, invoked the devil to help him. The devil consulted with the builder and promised to help finish the work, but the price would be the first soul to pass over the bridge. The builder consented and the work went along rapidly. Soon the bridge neared completion. Its beauty appealed to all who saw it. The builder, tremendously pleased with himself and with the bridge's reception, had forgotten about the devil's bargain until the devil reappeared.

"I have come for my soul," the devil told the builder. "Tomorrow, when the bridge opens, I will take the first soul that crosses."

The builder, who was a clever man by all accounts, had a day to decide what to do. At first he believed it only fair to sacrifice himself. After all, he had made the bargain with Satan; it was he who should honor it. Then he thought of sending an old person who did not have much business left on earth, or perhaps one of the mentally infirm who might, by their confusion, be spared the understanding of what had occurred. No one had been permitted to cross the bridge. The builder posted guards to prevent it from occurring.

The builder, so filled with dread he could not sleep, came to his morning coffee not knowing what to do. He asked God for a sign, though he did not believe God would interfere with the devil's work. He spoke softly to his wife. He had not told her what Satan required, but he could not be certain he would see her again. He kissed his boy on the forehead, ruffled the youngster's hair, and walked slowly toward the bridge.

He made one stop to buy bread. As he tucked the bread inside his shirt, a dog began to follow him. Many dogs roamed the street in Lucca and at first the builder took little notice. But then, as he neared the bridge, an idea came to him.

"I am ready to pay my debt," he announced to the devil.

The builder told the guards to stand aside.

"Very well," said the devil, "give me my soul."

With that, the builder drew the bread and waved it in front of the dog. When the dog could hardly contain itself, the builder threw the loaf across the bridge. The dog sprinted after the bread and the devil, bested by a mere builder who had remembered at the last moment that a human soul had never been stipulated, accepted the dog's soul and disappeared. The dog, too, vanished, but the bridge remained and may be crossed today without fear and with much admiration for its lovely shape. The dog's name was not known and therefore could not be forgotten.

The white starlight created by Laika's capsule burning in our atmosphere was the trace of a dog chasing bread across a bridge, and human flight the beauty left behind.

Mary came back around eleven, and we all pitched in to clean sap buckets. We were still a couple weeks away from tapping trees for maple syrup, but Fred said he wanted to get the equipment ready. The buckets were a little sticky from the sap the year before. Mary washed, I dried, and Fred stacked them back down in the basement.

"I like it," Mary said when Fred carried a stack downstairs.

"Like what?"

She looked at me.

She liked the absence of nose studs.

We looked at each other.

"That's because you're incredibly square, Mary," I said.

Mary laughed. I had never seen her truly laugh. She put her head back and laughed from the belly. I didn't mean it to be so funny, but I could see now that it was.

Almost the second she stopped laughing, the phone rang.

Cindy smelled like peaches.

I sat in the passenger side of the Jetta, driving south. It was one o'clock.

We were supposed to meet my mother at four.

"How are you feeling?" Cindy asked when we finally got on the interstate.

I shrugged.

"It will be okay," she said.

"It feels weird."

"Well, I guess that's understandable."

"It happened fast."

Cindy looked at me. She shrugged.

"People use the term *alcoholic*, but not many people are just alcoholics," Cindy said. "It's a type of personality. Heavy drinking, maybe some drugs, tobacco. It adds up."

"And poor choices in men?"

Cindy pursed her lips. Nodded.

"Probably," she said.

The afternoon passed by the car windows gray and calm. The radio said snow later. The Jetta heater worked too hard for a while, then, when Cindy cut it back, it got chilly inside.

"So who is this guy?" I asked.

"Her boyfriend. Cooper. That's what she calls him. Steve said he seemed nice enough. The house is a bit out of control. A lot of stuff around. That's why I wanted us to meet at a restaurant. A neutral ground."

"How did she look?"

Cindy looked at me.

"A little the worse for wear, I guess. I don't know. Steve didn't spend a lot of time talking about that. She's skinny. Maybe too thin."

"And she's working at a convenience store?"

Cindy nodded.

"Did she ask about me?"

"Sure she did. But Steve doesn't really know you, does he? She agreed right away to meet you. That's why it happened so fast. That's a good sign. She didn't hem and haw."

"She's thirty-seven."

"That's right."

"How old is this Cooper guy?"

Cindy shook her head. She didn't know.

"Older," she said.

Whenever I go south, I can't shake the feeling that I am traveling downhill. When I go north, uphill. It doesn't matter how I approach it rationally. Down in my gut that's what I feel.

A long long time ago I lived inside my mother's belly. That was all I could think about. We once shared a heartbeat. We once took no breath except that it was shared between us.

Cindy pulled into the parking lot of an Applebee's.

"Everyone likes Applebee's," she said.

It was a joke. She looked at me.

"This one time, if you'd like a cigarette, I guess it would be okay."

"Here in the car?" I asked.

She nodded.

"You are the finest human being who ever lived," I said. "The queen of the universe."

She laughed. "Go ahead," she said.

I smoked with the window down on my side. Cindy looked to see if she could spot my mom. She looked at her watch. It was like my mom to be late. And it was possible she was already in the restaurant.

"As a general rule," Cindy said, "would you rather be in a restaurant and wait for a person, or walk in and be the person the other person is waiting for?"

"You're daft," I said.

"Answer."

"It can be good or bad either way," I said, not tasting the smoke, not tasting anything. My mouth worked, but I hardly knew what I was saying.

"For a date, I like to be the one sitting and waiting. That way you can see the other person walk in and you can check them out."

"And you can have a drink," I said.

"Okay, that too. Under other circumstances, I like to be the one coming in. If, say, I'm selling something. A house or whatever. I like the other person to think I'm busy and they'd better take me seriously. You know."

"Geez, you've thought about this stuff," I said.

She smiled."Ready to check it out inside?" she asked.

"Sure."

"Chin up and all that. You're a good person, Baby. Keep that in mind."

When I opened the car door, snow fell in white lines, drifting like clouds falling apart.

•

The evening special was prime rib, mashed potatoes, corn, garden salad.

Margaritas $2.75.

Jimmy Buffet played the song about stepping on a pop-top.

The hostess's name was Marge.

The Celtics played the Lakers on the TV above the bar. Celtics up by three.

My mother wasn't there.

Cindy said, "Let me just call her cell."

She took a few steps away and pulled out her phone. We stood near the hostess's stand. A few other people waited for tables. The hostess kept examining a seating chart, then looking at the people lined up. She seemed confused.

"She's not answering," Cindy said. "Why don't we get a table and have something to drink?"

I nodded.

Cindy said something quietly to Marge, the hostess.

"As fast as I can," Marge said.

Marge had gray hair with highlights the color of sky.

When the ice cracked under me, I had the strange sensation that I had been waiting for that instant my entire life. Odd, I know. But why else would a patch of ice break at the exact moment, in the exact way, that it did? It had to be fate. Just before the ice gave way, I felt the surface spring. It went down and up, and for a second it felt like running on a soft mattress. I didn't fear the water so much as I feared the ice pushing away. I did not fear falling so much as not being held up.

•

"Try not to take it so hard," Cindy said. "She isn't doing this to you. Not really. She just can't quite cope with things."

I held my head in my hands and cried. I had been crying for a long time.

"We should go," Cindy said. "I'm sorry, Baby."

I nodded. But I kept my head in my hands.

The waitress came over and asked if everything was okay. I suppose people had noticed us.

"Just the check, please," Cindy said quietly.

I knew the waitress hurried. Knew Cindy and she had exchanged a look. She came back fast. Cindy had her wallet out and put down a ten for our two sodas.

"Okay," Cindy said.

We stood. I kept my face down and followed her out.

Snow fell and the parking lot had turned white. I lifted my face to the flakes. If you stared up long enough, you could see the clouds above.

"I'm sorry," Cindy said.

"Not your fault," I said. My voice wobbled.

I climbed in the car.

23

I knew visiting Bobby was the booby prize, the thing you get when you don't get the real prize you want. I hadn't been able to see my mother, so they hurried around and got me a visitation with Bobby. I knew what they were doing, but that was okay.

You watch so many TV shows you expect prison to be one way when it's really another. Bobby wasn't behind a window, and he didn't have to use a phone. He just came into a small gray waiting room. He wore jeans and a prison-issue shirt. He had grown a goatee and looked thinner, more mature.

He kissed me on the cheek and then looked at Cindy.

"I'll give you a few minutes," she said.

I felt like I wanted to cry, then it passed. I sat. Bobby sat next to me. I didn't feel like I would cry quite so easily ever again.

"I heard," he said. "I'm sorry."

"One of those things."

"It sucks, though."

I nodded.

"How are *you* doing?" I asked.

"It's not bad," he said. "Not as bad as you would think. It's a kind of life, I guess."

"Good."

"And I've had good reports so far. They give you reports every week. You know, to keep track. I've had good behavior. All good."

"Nice," I said.

He grabbed my hand. "In some ways, Baby, it might be good your mom left again without seeing you."

I laughed. It was a short, hard laugh. I didn't mean it to be, but it came out anyway. "How do you figure?" I asked.

"Well, it's like she's either all in, or she should just stay away. You know what I mean? If she wasn't back for the long haul, maybe she figured it wasn't fair to give you any expectations."

"You're daft," I said.

"Maybe," he said. "But maybe she was trying to do something good for you. You could think of it that way."

Cindy had said something along the same lines when she found my mom had left. It made a certain abstract sense, but it still didn't feel very good. It let my mom off too easily. Gave her too much credit.

"You don't just have children and walk away from them," I said.

"I know."

We didn't say anything else for a while. Then I asked him a question. "When you get out of here, are you going to live legal?"

"What do you mean?"

"You know what I mean," I said. "Are you going to get a job and do what you need to do? Not sell drugs, not look for an easy way? Because that's what I think my mom did all her life. She looked for the easy way."

"I'm going to be different," he said.

And I knew he probably wouldn't be. And I knew my mom wouldn't be. And knew none of us ever changed except a tiny bit here and there, except when it helped, except when changing got something our original selves needed.

Bobby and I kissed. He started it and I went along with it. Deep down, way back in our hearts, we knew we kissed just for form. It was some sort of step we had to take. That old gut tingle I used to feel with Bobby wasn't there.

Cindy came in a little later. I knew we were both relieved to see her. Bobby and I hugged. Then Cindy led me out. We passed lots of hallways and cages. They didn't look like cages, but they were. They were rooms with small windows and thick doors and wire mesh on the glass. I looked at them and I thought of dump dogs. The guys locked up in the cages had stayed too long at the dump, had eaten too greedily. When everything was said and done, that was their real crime.

Nicky came home for his birthday. I helped Mary bake his favorite cake—white cake, white icing, and coconut flakes. She called it Snowball Cake. We had fresh pasta for dinner, a salad, and the dessert. Sebastian got to sit at the table and wear a party hat. We all wore those silly paper hats, but Sebastian kept pawing his off. Fred took pictures. Nicky was twenty-nine.

Afterward we played Scrabble and I finished third. I had trouble sitting close to Nicky. He was that handsome. He came with Fred and me to feed the dogs. He was good around the dogs, natural and easy. The dogs liked him.

I don't know if it was Fred or Nicky, but someone suggested we take the dogs out for a run. A big moon had come up, and Nicky said it wasn't to be missed. He said he would run one team, I could run the other. Fred volunteered to stay at base and catch us when we returned.

We rigged up. Nicky harnessed Fred's team and I harnessed mine. Mary came out and held lines. We lined them out side by side, and Fred counted us down. Nicky went first. I counted to a hundred, then nodded to Fred and Mary. They stepped aside and my dogs shot into the woods.

It was different to run at night. The snow shone blue and the trees appeared like dark overcoats suspended on hangers. I did not pump very much. The dogs seemed strong and willing, as though this was a treat they hadn't anticipated. I chanted my dog chant to Laika. She ran beautifully, the bones of her shoulders flexing and pulling. The other dogs galloped with her. At times I lost sight of the dogs altogether. I rode two runners through the snow and the woods passed beside me.

Only once before the finish did I see Nicky's team. He ran through a gap in the trees, heading up an incline. The moon happened to fit right behind him, like a penny rolling down the hill he climbed. It was more than pretty to see him. He looked as though he might lift right into the sky.

I held onto the handlebar and then, for a while, nothing separated me from the sled. It sounds crazy, I know, but that's how I felt. My legs and hands seemed to grow into the sled and I did not feel any separation. But then I continued to float forward, to leave the sled and earth and become a team member. Not the fastest. Not the strongest. But I ran beside the dogs, my heart hooked to theirs, my stride their stride, their breath my breath. This was my pack, maybe my only pack. To run through the woods under a full moon filled my heart with longing and with hope.